URIK -TAH, THE DEATH ROSE

Majesty's Final Voyage

Lance K. Steele

Copyright © 2011

ALL RIGHTS RESERVED

ISBN# 978-09827031-5-1

FOR INFORMATION CONTACT

lanceksteele@yahoo.com

"One cannot think Universe...

Without also thinking God"

I hope you like my first venture into science fiction. In college, I dabbled in the life sciences; biology, physiology, chemistry and physics. But of all the lessons learned, one stood out most of all. It seems that in every field of science, when you finally get to its cutting edge, you will ultimately stumble upon God.

In physics we see oppositely charged particles, which ought to be repelling each other, yet they don't; what holds them together? "Glue." That's the best they can come up with, for such a glaring paradox.

In orthopedics we see fractured bone ends approximating each other that should heal, but sometimes don't. The micro-voltage needed for fusion is 3-4 Gauss; precisely the same voltage as that generated by the earth itself. In chiropractic we often see incredible healings and yet sometimes we can't explain or duplicate them in other patients with the same condition, even though they get the same treatment protocol.

Surgeons do their thing; when the patient gets well, the surgeon takes the credit. But when there are complications they say; "It's in God's hands."

Every scientific experiment ever performed has to begin sometime. It also must begin with certain tools, elements and a working hypothesis. This is the very basis of science.

It's how scientists derive data... and draw logical conclusions.

Even in the coldest realms of science, such as astronomy, the biggest questions of all come down to the same thing. For example, question number one; where did the universe come from? Big Bang? Please... Don't insult yourself.

First law of physics; matter cannot be created or destroyed. One cannot 'bang' nothing and get something.

That's what makes our study of space so preposterous; we begin with these huge, insoluble enigmas, then we try to solve the infinite with finite brains.

Why we continue to deny
the existence
of God

is perhaps the biggest
sci-fi mystery
of all.

DISCLAIMERS

Everything in this book is fictional. Any proper name, place or event that might coincidentally align itself with a real one *is... unintentional.* It's fiction, *got it?*

Likewise, anything that looks like plagiarism isn't... It's just that I've read Sci-Fi books, watched movies and TV sci-fi for many years... so there's bound to be some unintentional bleed over from my subconscious onto the pages of this tome. Hell; I grew up watching the original Star Trek, Twilight Zone, Outer Limits, et cetera. So don't panic if I unintentionally leaked a bit of trivia.

OH, yeah; there's one more disclaimer. It's in the after-word. But for now, kindly step onto the bridge of the finest starship in the Federation's fleet. So sit down, buckle in, and shut the hell up.

CONTENTS

DON'T HATE ME...
If the page count'S off. *Find a better reason!*
Online publishing's page count is the bane of my
existence.

TO DISCOVERY...
WHEREVER
YOU MIGHT
FIND IT

ONE...

DECEL

Starship Commander Theodore R. Morgan came out of space sleep precisely on schedule, just half a sector from step-down. All around him the other officers' pods began opening; his senior staff knew the drill; no scratching, yawning or whining. So they stretched, smiled as if they felt all right and then they each went into the evo-con scanner for precautionary decontamination.

True, there hadn't been a space-sleep genetic contamination for over twenty EASY, but that last incident in the Rijel sector was enough to keep everybody gun-shy about evocon hopovers. Fifty-two dead, with another dozen permanently disfigured bad enough that they had to be euthanized in the PDI to avoid replicating their errors.

Ted Morgan shuddered at the thought of dying in the Plasma Digital Inverter Beam. It had to feel like being shredded into a billion burning pieces, and then getting tossed into a laser beam of unimaginable intensity, and finally having your billions of bits cast to the vastness of open space. He forced the grisly thoughts from his mind as senior staff members took their stations.

" I trust you had a good sleep, Will?"

"Yes, thank you, sir... And yourself?"

"Fine, thank you... begin step-down to Hawk three, on my mark."

The whole staff gasped at the faux pas.

"Hawk *THREE* Sir? Might I remind; we're currently at *SIX*, half a Q from Zero Light?"

Morgan quickly nodded assent.

"Thank you, number one... Damned those sleep echoes, anyhow! Begin sequential step-down, *quickly.*"

"Rapid decel... AYE, SIR."

Harder was glad the old man wasn't stubborn; there was no time to debate his fatal choice. Any braking of more than two Hawkins levels would surely prove fatal. No vertebrate species could survive such extreme decel, assuming the ship herself could survive it.

William Harder punched the button and the ship went into invo-linear braking, already knowing it was no place for expo... That damned exponential braking was a real ball breaker. The last time they used it, his scrotum felt like a Parsep ball after sudden death period.

Fortunately, everybody's G-comp stations worked well enough to survive the real-time, two hundred- fifty G braking rate. Ship's gunner, Little Rija, kept right on eating her remanufactured pastry, totally oblivious to the massive starship's extreme effort to slow the fuck down.

In less than half a quark, Majesty transitioned to Low-Warp and finally slowed to light speed. The crew always liked that part, seeing the pretty ribbons of white, red and sometimes burgundy, if they were close to a good nebula. Regrettably, the Hayfork Nebula was too far aft for the retro screens to visualize. So this slow-down was boring; just a thousand or so star-ribbons, this being a sparsely starred sector. Then she bogged down to sub-light, when they could finally exit their G-comp stations and walk about freely.

Just as they slowed again to impulse velocity, the forward monitor lit up. Onto the lower right section popped their destination, Ala Sphenoidis Nine. Rija Patel gasped; she was the only senior staff to see it for the first time. By Captain's orders to preserve her sense of discovery, no one could foretell her about it; the woman was entitled.

Admittedly, it *was a bizarre oddity;* the entire Ala Sphenoidis system was one of only three in the charted universes having non-spheroid planets. The Ala planetoids had Bat-wing appendages, hence the Primitive, pre-blast-Earth Latin monikers to describe them.

Ala Nine was typical of the other Bat-wings, having large spatulated ends extending from its thorax-like center. It did sort of resemble a huge oddly spinning space-bat.

Carol Three Feathers, first Native American replicant to grace a bridge, had seen it before. As far as she cared; seen one, you've seen 'em all.

"Sir, I'm not picking up any sign of human life. It's still pretty far, but I'm not reading colonials, sir."

The head of security, Three Feathers never took a moment off. Morgan chose her because she was always about the job. Still, at one-fourth Quark distance, it was doubtful that even the Majesty's superp far-sensors could pick up heartbeats, EEG or Pineal Gland bio-rad from something as tiny as humans.

"Very well; keep me posted. Ensign Bok-Tah, slow to one-tenth impulse, full magnification on Ala Nine and step up the micro shields please. Those damnable rocks are giving me a headache."

El-Tar Bok-Tah, the Poov-Ran, acknowledged.

"Quarter limp, full-mag, boosting deflectors, aye."

Morgan eyed the kid suspiciously; top of the academy, but always looked like he'd stolen something. Perhaps it was the fact that the Poov-

Ran had been cunning, vindictive enemies just twenty EASY ago...

Morgan destroyed many a Poov Death-Frigate, back then. Still, IG FED desegregation mandated; ten percent of staff be Poov-Ran, so he hired the best and kept and kept a sharp eye on them... After all, twenty Earth Atmosphere Standard-Orbit Years wasn't a very long time, when it came to enemies; converted or otherwise.

But he didn't have long to worry about old enemies, as new ones kept pounding the shields; monster micrometeors, some as big as human heads, were common in the Ala system. At extreme velocities, such a meteor could wreak more damage than a Lividian phaser burst. The current barrage sounded more like billiard ball-sized particles.

He hated the Ala Sphenoidis system. Were it not for its vast composite resources, Morgan would have loved to just blast it all away. Back when he was a rogue, he used to love to go out and shoot desolate systems, just to watch the planets pop.

Ah, but that was before IG Fed took him under its wing, teaching him the value of desolate systems... and combat... and finally, diplomacy. Still, it was hard to resist the urge to just smoke this system and its polymer resources, for no other reason than the fun of watching it smoke off into open space.

"Little Rija, is there any way you can shoot down those damnable micros?"
She jumped at the chance to play with her phasers.
"Aye, sir... targeting at once, Sir."

They were impossible to hit, but anything was better than staring at the ugly misshapen planet, since it didn't take her long to be bored with it. Soon the rhythmical background hum of cadenced phaser fire pulsed through the bridge. An electronic heartbeat, signifying multiple bursts from the smallest phaser array; the anionic phasers... each blast the equivalent of a 90-million mega joule planet killer. She would have preferred smaller phasers for the agile work, but Majesty had nothing smaller.

Of course, the commander knew she couldn't hit the meteors; they were made up of carbon fibers, just like the Ala Sphenoidis planets... incredibly fine, long willowy fibers, some eighty meters long on the planets, but mere inches long on these micro-meteors.

These fibers were so fine that they couldn't be reproduced in zero-grav labs. It was their purity and extreme strength-to-weight characteristic that drew so many races to the Ala system. And their stealth qualities, while nobody spoke of them, certainly spoke for themselves... Ala Sphenoidis carbon fibers were not only invisible to old-school radar, sensor arrays and EMR... they also canceled tritium turbulence and cold-filtered positron trails; essential traits if one wanted to cloak a warship from the best high-tech prying eyes in the known galaxies. Truly, Ala carbon was the good shit.

This made targeting the meteors impossible; you can't hit what you can't see. But it kept the gunner occupied, so everybody was happy, and

Rija could be such a bitch without something to shoot at. That's what made it so surprising...

"Woa... you *GOT ONE!*" Three Feathers was as shocked as Rija.

"How did you do that?"

Little Rija shrugged.

"I noticed stars blinking out in a straight line; had to be a stealth rock trajectory, so I eyeballed it." She was pleased with herself.

Pretty soon, micrometeors began poofing fairly often, once she got the proper lead for the little stealth bombs. It wasn't as accurate as Majesty's ballistic-tracking apps, but they were useless against carbon. Rija was the only game in town.

She started enjoying it. The ones she missed made a hell of a bang on the distal perimeter shield. Nobody had a clue that Rija's new target tracking trick might pay off in the future. They were just glad she was happy.

Ensign El-Tar Bok-Tah caught his attention.

"Sir, we're now at far-orbit and still, I don't see ANY signs of life."

They were well within sensor range, so the screen should be crammed with biomag signals. Ted Morgan was a lifelong student of archival cuss-words in three galaxies; he felt the urge to call one up from his native Earth's pre-blast lexicon... *'bullshit.'* But he exercised restraint.

"Most unexpected indeed... Captain Harder, we shall send a team to the planet; please wake up four security officers and a medic."

 "Aye Sir, right away."

He flicked a switch and five more pods lit up. In ten minutes the search team would be ready. These crew members were space-sleeping far aft of the bridge, so when they awoke, they could scratch, bitch and fart as they liked.

Just then Carol Three Feathers swore in Firsi.

"Tek noh semble!"

She and the Commander were the only ones that knew Firsi and he was surprised she knew it well enough to say *"fuck my own ass"* with such clear diction and accent.

"Security... What's the source of your surprise?"

"Tek no semble... Sir, I'm picking up... WATER, sir.... *WATER!*"

"Impossible! Re-confirm sensors, Lieutenant."

"Aye, sir... recalibrating now."

The entire staff stood mesmerized at the thought of water on the black powder planet. Even Little Rija quit shooting meteors.

"Uh... Sir, sensors still confirm... Ala Nine is showing a freshwater lake, approximately two kilometers by one-half, essentially dead-center in the core... and, Sir? There's something more."

"What could possibly be 'more' than a lake?"

"Well, sir, there is life in it, Sir... *life forms.*"

Rija powered down the phasers and the bridge went silent at the thought of life.

"Well, we certainly need time to study this. Ensign, put us into thruster-assisted orbit, and be sure to compensate for those damnable spinning wings. I want a minimum clearance of 100,000 kilometers."

"100K clearance, thrust-assist, aye, sir."

The mammoth ship obeyed, taking an oblong synthetic orbit, full sensors scanning the planet. All sensors, that is, except security's, which scanned non-stop for danger; one never knew when those bastards would drop cloaks... She hated Carnelians and their cowardly attacks.

And even though their claim was staked on Ala Fourteen, they weren't above raiding other mines if the chance presented. And yet, this didn't look like the work of Carnelians, but it still paid to be vigilant.

Meanwhile, science officer Tutok full-scanned the planet for two full orbits.
"Commander Morgan, I confirm initial observations; there appears to be a freshwater lake, average depth sixteen meters. I'm getting mixed readings of lower life-form in and around the lake, but nothing on the rest of the surface, sir."
This didn't surprise Morgan; their sensors rarely worked perfectly on carbonized planets, thanks to the damnable carbon dust floating on solar winds.

"And sir, the mining colony seems to be... gone."

Tutok played with adjustments on the touch-panel.

"Searching for signs of violence."

A short scan ensued.

"I see no evidence of conventional weapon attacks as we know them, sir; no Chimura scorches to indicate Lividian phaser burns... no pinch bomb di-tritium sulfite trace, so clearly the Carnelians did not destroy them. I'm not reading positron levels, ionic pulse scars or matrix shadowing to indicate any known conventional weaponry. It looks like the miners just... left, sir."

Just then Tutok amended his opinion.

"Strike that; picking up traces of cadaverine and putrescene on the west wing, sir."

Morgan wasn't surprised at that, either; no signs of life, plus no proof that they left equals dead miners. But how could they *all* have died?

"Scanning friendly air, Tutok?"

"Affirm, sir; atmo is homogeneous... 60, 16, 24... we can breathe it for several hours, sir."

"There's no *"we"*, Tutok... you're not going. I need you here. Doctor Frasier-ak-Maheed, scan your list; see if any of the away team can't take 24 percent carbon dioxide for two hours."

Debrinda Frasier-ak-Maheed snapped to. She was on her last mission; wanted to end it with a bang. "Aye, sir, scanning; the Vorr cannot tolerate ambient Plus Four."

He withered at the thought; Tam and Rak of the Vorr colony, were his two bravest and strongest warriors, dedicated only to the Commander. Without Vorr, his team would be sorely compromised if they encountered hostiles.

"Very well. Make ready the away team, and keep the Vorr aboard. Officer Tutok, please scan for cloaks."

"Aye sir, already done; there is a ninety-six percent chance that NO cloaks are on this planet. There is a ninety-five percent that no cloaks are within immediate vessel attack range."

"Very well, we'll have to live with a four-percent chance of annihilation. Make ready four marines of your choosing, Carol."

"Aye, sir; I'll take Hardbody, Caps, Juneau and Winford."

Tutok pressed the button and those four pods lit up. The Marines began to stir.

Fifteen minutes later, senior staff sat in the war room to brief the away team. Commander Morgan entered and sat down; "This recon will be swift and to the point. Our mission is to ascertain the status of the 245 miners and their 22 children, to determine if they are living cloaked or were killed or forcibly taken from Ala Nine. Our secondary goal is improvisational... although I haven't yet contacted IG Fed, I am confident they'll be more than curious about this... *LAKE* we're reading. Perhaps it's linked to the miners' fate."

"The last goal is to determine if Ala Nine is safe for a replacement colony; we can't let it sit empty; by the time IG Fed sponsors another colony, the Carnelians could establish squatter's rights. I have already dispatched a buoy signal to Federation for replacement miners, so assuming it's safe to re-inhabit, we will have to orbit and defend until they arrive. Now, I don't like babysitting planets any more than the rest of you, but those are the goals. Any questions?"

Carol raised a hand.

"Sir, the life forms in the lake; do we kill them?"

He nodded and raised his eyebrows.

"Well, clearly we *can kill them* if we wish. The Imperial Directive has been waived here, since there was NO LIFE before we brought it...so that makes all life on that planet ours to do with as we deem necessary. You may kill at your discretion, but the emphasis *IS...* discretion. I don't want anyone phasing space cucumbers again, is that clear?"

The group spoke in unison.

"Clear, sir...aye."

"Remember, just because something looks slimy and ugly... is not reason enough to shoot.... So it's Defense of Life and Property only, got it?"

The team chanted together.

"DLP, AYE, SIR."

Tutok grimaced at the thought of space cukes getting blasted. They sure did stink when phasered. Ugly little buggers, but so friendly; and who would think that such slimy little turd-looking slugs could make so much pure oxygen? Anyway, Defense of Life and Property protocol was in play, so there would be no varmint shooting on this trip.

The away team hit the transport platform with full gear, phasers and body armor. Ten seconds later the cargo bay was empty, save for the sickeningly sweet odor of the PDI transporter beams slowly dissipating.

TWO...

MISSION

The six-man team consisted of Carol Three Feathers, her four best grunts; Hardbody, Caps, Juneau and Winford... And of course, Science Officer Tutok, who somehow managed to convince Morgan to let him beam down. They landed precisely one inch above the planet surface, and when the Plasma Digitizing Inverter beams died away, everyone dropped an inch to the surface with surprised looks on their faces.

Tutok alone remained un-surprised; he hated beaming onto composite planetoids with their stealthy, hard to scan surfaces, the horrible solar winds and carbon dust ghosting... but he was glad the sensor misread was only an inch this time. The last time it was fourteen meters. That drop killed his away team, leaving only Tutok to survive... And that was at the cost of three lumbar vertebral fractures, lacerations in two of his livers, and a broken mandible. True, two days under the replicator beam restored him perfectly, but the pain burned heavily into his memory. He hated composite planetoids. And, for a science officer to hate anything was a rare thing, indeed.

The air was fairly breathable, with approximately 16 percent oxygen and 24% CO_2. The remainder was nitrogen and a few other lesser Royal Inerts common to this part of the galaxy. Tutok knew their names well enough; Sulftitium, Trilithial Xenon and Pharosmotia, mostly. Although they were inert to humanoids, and barely perceptible even with the best e-sniffers, they were absolutely lethal to Exoskeletals.

That fact alone kept him content; he hated those etoid beetle-like exo's ever since they pillaged his home planet and ate his entire family tree. There was only one benefit from the Exoskeletal raid; it forced the young Tutok to devote his life to invent a way to kill the entire race; in the process, he became one of the premiere science officers in IG Fed history.

At any rate, he couldn't lure an entire Exoskeletal race into an eclipse xenon trap, although he'd schemed and designed for decades; the Exoskels were far too wary for such a child's trap to work. They had sniffers specifically dedicated to sniff all gasses that might dissolve their shells. So, although Tutok's day might never come, he remained hopeful and vigilant. If he ever got the chance, he'd kill them all... and the Federation's Imperial Directive be damned.

Carol Three Feathers reacted first to the unexpected one-inch free-fall.

"But the fuck was that?"

Without the commander present, she felt secure in trying a few of his pet archival Earth cusswords.

Tutok answered.

"That... the fuck... was the result of carbon-dust affecting Majesty's sensors; don't worry, it won't affect our PDI return trip. Might I suggest we find the missing colonials immediately?"

"You got it. I hate this place already! Juneau, Winford, you're on point. Hardbody, Caps, bring up the rear. The sooner we learn what happened, the sooner we get off this Etoid rock."

The marines spoke and acted as one.

"Aye, sir."

Their phasers ready-swept the perimeter while the away team searched buildings and out-sheds.

They found nothing other than microscopic traces indicating that the miners probably died on-site. Everything else looked normal; no sign of warship attack, no damage to structures or life support systems. After four hours of intense searching, the team uploaded their final findings to Majesty on a secure pulse-modulated frequency. The response came instantly, which surprised nobody; Majesty probably knew this information already, given her superior sensor capability. The keyed message hit the com-pak readout.

"Hold fast. Will PDI team to lake."

"Everybody, hold still; we're transporting to the lake."

Ten seconds later all that remained was the sickening smell of the PDI beams.

They popped out, facing a most unimaginable sight. Only Three Feathers had seen a lake before. It looked so unreal... so much shimmering water in one spot. To the marines, it looked as unnatural as a huge mountain made up of diamonds or Tuterium crystals.

Tutok knew wild water. He'd seen it before in quantities larger than a bio-bag, but this amount of water practically blew his rational mind to shit. He pointed his scanner at it. One second later, data hit his screen. Five seconds later he was still pointing, mesmerized. Three Feathers kicked him out of his reverie.

"What you got?"

Tutok startled out of his mini-trance.

"Sensors confirm Majesty's prior readings... fresh water and completely... *DRINKABLE!*" The team gasped at the thought. Such decadence; to drink wild water that had never been through a recycler... it was too much to contemplate.

The marines were first to adapt.

Three Feathers heard noises, turned and saw Harbideau and Caps stripping down to shorts...

"Hardbody, the fuck what are you doing?"

Harbideau always spoke for all four grunts.

"Disrobing... ma'am. We're paid to take risks, improvise, overcome and adapt."

Before she could react, all four marines were bare-ass naked; they strode to the shoreline with unbelievable boldness. She watched those four white, muscular bodies moving and something inside her went unexpectedly white-hot.

Maybe it was their total fearlessness of whatever dangers might be lurking under the surface; she knew that marines felt no fear, but this was too much to imagine.

They hit the water simultaneously, four naked asses wide. It phosphoresced and splashed when their ankles entered... little jewels splashing up around their legs. Winford turned around to call Tutok and Three Feathers. His penis stood at full attention.

"It feels... great! It's water! *Come on!*"

The rigid penis was something she'd never seen before; it looked odd, but strangely, *good*. Just then the scent hit her; pheromones from four of the most masculine bodies she'd ever been close to... and that was bad enough. But the other scents vied for attention.

Never before had she smelled mud oozing with minor life forms and rotting organisms. Then there was the odor of wild water. This new scent was the most intoxicating, erotic smell she'd ever encountered. Before she knew it, Carol Three Feathers, of Earth's ancient ancestral Cherokee lineage, stood naked as hell, ass-deep in the lake. Her nipples erected and her neck sex-blushed passionately. Her first-ever orgasm hit her amidships. She cried silently, just standing there feeling so many uncharted emotions, standing next to four naked marines and a fish-cold, four-eyed, three-livered science officer. At that moment she could've fucked them all... and been court-martialed a happy woman.

Hardbody spoke next; "Sir, my feet are sinking. We should get out... now."

Not knowing what evils might lurk in the ooze, all five explorers reluctantly got out. They walked to their clothes slowly, each person absorbed in the emotion of the bizarre moment. Wherever the liquid had touched them, the breezes now coated wet skin with ultra-fine carbon powder.

From the waist down, the entire away team was the same color; black. It was strangely erotic for the whole team to be monochromatic from the genitals down. Tutoks' normal pale green Tahetan pallor, Three Feathers' reddish brown integument, even the Marines' bilirubin-enhanced space-sleep white-pink... were all the same; jet black.

The scene brought them together... Six people, whose origins spanned four billion light years, whose ancestors never even saw light from the others' suns... whose very DNA implied separation, were suddenly monochromatically equal. That such a moment transpired in the presence of wild water in abundance was no surprise to anyone who knew the universe.

Water is life. It is also color-less.

They sat down to get dressed. Caps twitched.
"Hey, what's this?"
A single leech sucked greedily from his popliteal fossa... he couldn't see it, but he felt the tail wiggling. Tutok removed it with a tiny laser scalpel meant for dissection.

"It appears to be some sort of invertebrate exoparasite. Scanning now... yes, it's a typical gray leech variety... evo-con is clear... it's harmless by all counts, but we should check each other in case there are more."

Carol wanted to check the marines, but Tutok saved her from her obvious passion... it wouldn't look good on the Ship's Report to have any mention of illegal arousal.

"Ma'am, please turn around and I'll scan you for leeches. You marines, scan each other."
"Aye, sir... scanning leeches."

Once secure, they dressed and stood up, preparing to beam back to Majesty. They didn't know how to tell the commander about... wading in wild water. It was simply too decadent for description.

Tutok opened the communicator just when Winford noticed the rose.

"Oh, Mak-Tow, that's *BEAUTIFUL!*" Nobody heard Winford cuss before; they looked where he was pointing. The sight caught them all by surprise.

Less than ten meters to the east stood a spectacular lone red rose, of unimaginable beauty. To take one's eyes off it was virtually impossible. They moved as one to the rose. Tutok, normally objective about discovery, was only slightly less taken than the rest.

"Stand clear, until I scan, please."

But instead of the usual five-second scan, Tutok hit every spectrum. Sixty seconds elapsed while everyone else gazed at the flower.

"Well, it's a flower... But I have no record of such a plant in my sensor's database; perhaps Majesty's database does."

He uploaded the full-spectrum scan to Majesty. As they waited for the search results, Three Feathers couldn't stand it any more. Combined with the passion of wading in water, seeing the marines naked and everybody temporarily being black from the waist down, Three Feathers had a bad case of Space Rapture.

She breached Away Team protocol and touched the plant.

"It's so beautiful."

Just then the flower released its scent, which was indescribably attractive. Before Tutok could warn her, he too became enraptured; the scent soon had the whole team entranced.

Majesty's report came down. It was just a rose, and there were plenty more on the far side of the lake. Bio-scans confirmed Tutok's sensors; there were no defects, threats or contamination risks to humans, hybrids, clones or replicants. Aside from an unusually high amount of opiate-like substance in the stamen, the flower was quite typical of the famous Rose-Tulip cross from the

Nigel-Strauss Rift near the Septium Nebulus, approximately fifty thousand light-years away.

Reading the team's mind, Commander Morgan pre-empted the obvious question and downloaded his consent; yes, they could bring the flower aboard... for purely scientific reasons, of course. After all, Majesty *was* a science vessel.

Besides, Morgan liked opiates... being this deep in space's dark corners held advantages for high command. A few sniffs from a harmless plant could be a good thing.

Twelve minutes later, the PDI beamed the away team back, after just a few unusual, but momentary calibration glitches from the transporter panel. The engineer was not terribly alarmed at the glitches; she chalked it up to carbon dust, which often had a way of interfering with finely tuned equipment.

Had it occurred anywhere else in the galaxies, Sargent Sue Miller would have been concerned about the initial gene scan glitch, especially one occurring within the oleil security, spectral analysis sub-route systems. But at least this time, the whole team landed perfectly on the cargo bay floor, no bouncing, dropping or phantom beaming issues. And with them, the gorgeous rose sat happily on the deck... its roots enmeshed with mud-coated carbon fibers, lake ooze and a few wriggling gray leeches.

Knowing better than to blast the leeches, minor organisms and ooze, they re-scanned the rose and its muddy entourage. It was proper procedure; first find out what it needs before you kill, clean or wash away the infrastructure. The scan quickly verified; the rose was harmless, and it didn't need the leeches or muddy goop to survive; it would thrive with a standard hydroponics mix and full-spectrum open-space lighting protocols.

The autoscan followed I.D. procedure for preventing inter-space floral-faunal hijackers. It quickly exterminated the leeches and sterilized the ooze before beaming it four hundred kilometers into space. Then it logged the abatement with Ig-Fed's Imperial Directive Committee, to cover Majesty's ass in case anything went wrong later.

By the time the away team returned to their stations, the rose had a clean tray and a hydro-grow osmosis pack of saturation nutrients. It was squeaky clean and on its way to meet the Commander.

THREE...
URIK-TAH

When Science Officer Tutok stepped onto the bridge with the rose, every officer gasped. Even Ted Morgan, a man who'd seen plenty of beauty couldn't refrain from exclamation. He forgot his vow to refrain from archival profanity.

"Damn it, man... that's the prettiest flower I've ever seen!"

They crowded close for a better view; the rose released its universal pheromone lure. It took less than ten seconds to intoxicate the senior crew. Carol Three Feathers spoke first.

"Smells fantastic too, but on the surface it smelled even... *better*, if that's possible."

Tutok interjected to keep speculation from getting out of control.

"On the surface we had high CO_2 and Royal Inerts to heighten olfaction. Aboard Majesty, we're breathing standard IG Fed air, which impairs smell. Curiously however, it *smells better than it should.*"

Morgan shrugged. He was eager to get the rose to chambers where he could try the opiates.

"Very well. Please make arrangements to keep it safe in the science lab for assessment; I'm sure that Intergalactic Federation will be more than interested, since we've never before encountered this species. But first I'd like a few moments to admire it in private. Beam it to my chambers."

"Private chambers, aye, sir."

Once alone with the rose, Morgan made the most of it. He first tried to open a petal, but they were clamped tightly, so he threaded a tiny wire between them, fished around and hit the stamen. The wire came out with a tiny bit of opiate residue.

The moment it got close to his nose, the opiate leaped from the wire to his nostrils; Morgan immediately felt total bliss. It bordered on the spectacular orgasms he'd had on Probius three, virtually beyond description in any language.

It didn't seem to last long; four minutes, maybe. He couldn't be sure, because the sensation had been so overpowering. When he came down he was disoriented.

"Computer, give me the correct time, please."

"Aye, Commander... shall it be ship's time, solar, voyage, IG-Fed or EASY time, sir?"

"Ship's time, please."

"Aye, Commander; Six twenty-two point four."

Morgan was amazed; apparently, his 'four-minute high was twenty minutes long.

"Computer, enable security cloak."

"Confidential cloak engaged, sir."

"How long was I immobile?"

"Aye, sir; the Commander entered REM sleep point-four seconds after inhaling pollen... transitioned to parabolic Delta wavelength for duration, sir... Reestablishing normal REM point-four seconds before resuming operational consciousness, sir."

He shook his head in astonishment; it was the fastest, purest rush of all... No lag, letdown or hangover. Better yet, he felt clarity and freshness.

"Computer, scan my bio-rads please."

"Aye, sir... All biological radiations are optimal."

"Very well, disable security cloak."

"Aye, commander; personal log is re-enabled."

So that was it; a perfect opiate rose, giving a wonderful, short-term high, with no crash or health risk. Resisting the urge to take another fine wire biopsy, he ordered staff to take the rose to Science's specimen display wing.

He was one of the best commanders in IG Fed, partly due to his incredible willpower... and yet the rose tested him almost to his limit. Besides, there should be time to clone it... maybe keep one in his quarters.

Back on the bridge the staff had a hunch that he had been sniffing; he had a notorious weakness for opium, and besides, something about that rose already tweaked them all.

Duty Officer Meer announced him.

"Commander on Deck."

"Number One, status check."

"Sir... All systems normal. Away team is back and healthy, after ionic baths to purge planetary residues. And so far, we have yet to find any living colonials. It's fair to say they are all dead, sir, based upon multiple areas of trace decomp signal, sir."

"Very well, Number One... I'd like Inner Circle Officers in Tactics Room right away."

"Aye, sir; putting marines back to sleep. Top officers to tactics room at once, sir."

Inner Circle consisted of Ship's gunner Little Rija, William Harder, Carol Three Feathers, Tutok and Dr. Debrinda Frasier-ak-Maheed. They were seasoned in combat, protocol and were loyal beyond measure. When they were seated, Morgan began immediately.

"We've established the fact that no colonials survived. We have no evidence of Carnelian, Carnassian or Lividian attack, nor have we seen any signs of cloaks or pinch rays. Does anyone have anything to share?"

Debrinda Frasier-ak-Maheed nodded.

"Sir, perhaps we should deploy another buoy to IG Fed, then baby-sit the planet until the replacement colonials get here."

"Well, clearly we'll have to orbit and maintain a presence, so I think that's a given, Deb."

She was one of his oldest and trusted officers, as well as a friend. First names were appropriate.

"But damn it all, I do hate to baby-sit... any other suggestions?"

Tutok raised his eyebrows.

"Sir, there might be another option. We wouldn't have to wait so long for the new colonials if we could find an SSC nearby. There is a one-point-two percent chance of finding an aperture within serviceable range of Ala Nine... say, ten thousand light years or less."

Now Captain Harder raised his brows.

"Hmmm... that's a good idea. We could shop around, while still remaining within sensor range of Nine. If we were to get lucky, we could save months of baby-sitting. Then we could perhaps... find a place for some shore leave? However, we have no record of Subspace Conduits this far out."

"Sir, it's possible that a conduit might exist. When IG Fed first got the charter for Ala Nine, they searched diligently for conduits... But that was twenty-eight EASY ago, sir; I remind the Commander that side-scanning and cross-beam technology has improved a great deal since then... Perhaps we might find what they missed."

Morgan drooled at the thought of becoming a hero again. Clearly, anyone finding an SSC near such a great resource would be forever hailed an IG Fed hero.

"So if we go and search, what will it cost us?"

Three Feathers was quick to dampen the building enthusiasm.

"It will cost us *SECURITY*, sir... To scan for conduits would put the ship at risk! We'll need the lateral arrays at full power. Then we'll need our belly phasers fired at ninety degrees, to crossbeam the laterals if we want to see the distortion of a conduit. In order to do that, we will have to divert *all power from our cloak detectors... sir.*"

They all knew what that meant... While they were busy looking for the mythical SSC, they'd be cruising through space with their pants down. Any hostile warships could easily come in cloaked, get in their wake and shoot them to dust. They'd be dead before anyone felt the anion torpedo hit. Morgan chewed on it for several seconds before speaking.

"Well, the Carns still claim to be upholding their end of the truce, so if we can trust that, the risk is minimal. We haven't had any hits on our sensors in this system in ten EASY, so they might be as good as their word."

Rija rarely spoke, so everyone listened.

"Sir, with all due respect, it seems they're almost too calm. That's highly unlike the Carnelians I've fought before; if they're quiet, there's a reason for it. I wonder if..."

Harder's brainstorm interrupted her.
"Yes, they HAVE been quiet... Computer, run cargo grid, check Carnelian export logs, to and from Ala Sphenoidis Fourteen, please."

"Aye, Captain... exports are down eighty-one percent since last log, Ala system date 2456."

Tutok extrapolated the data and speculated.
"Sir, it's possible the Carnelians have discovered an SSC already. If they did, they'd want to keep it to themselves. That would explain why they're so quiet..."
Three Feathers supplemented the brainstorm.
"And they'd keep sending a few freighters, just to keep the neighbors from getting suspicious."
Harder was quick to truss the concept.
"We could approach Carn space, see what we..."

"Forget it, Number One. *If they HAVE* found a conduit I wouldn't want to risk an incident. IG Fed wouldn't back me on that play."

Tutok interjected.

"Sir, might I suggest an alternative? If we are to assume the Carnelians have found one, then the hunting ought to be even better for a secondary. Forty-five percent of all charted SSC's have ancillary tubes within two-point-five parseps. And since Ala Fourteen is only half a parsep from here..."

"Duly noted, Tahet, duly noted. We could be in prime territory for an auxiliary conduit, assuming that the Carnelians' drop in freighter traffic isn't due to some other factor. We can't trust anything involving Carnelians; they're almost as devious as the Emplois!"

The Inner Circle cringed at the image of the greasy, sleazy double-dealing, backstabbing little vermin. As primates went, Emplois were at the bottom rung of the ladder, an embarrassment to the entire field of galactic evoconvolution. If ever there were an exception to the Imperial

Directive's 'no species extinguished' clause, the Emplois would be it. For the commander to insinuate ethical proximity to the Emplois was the very zenith of insults.

As usual, Tahet Tutok posed the alternative.
"Or they could have found a better carbon fiber resource, perhaps closer to their home system. Or perhaps they discovered better stealth materials than carbon... Who can say? When it comes to Carnelians, *anything is possible."*

The group went silent in agreement; clearly the Carnelians were unpredictable and dangerous, even though they stayed friendly long enough to stake an Alar mining claim.

Ted Morgan hadn't risen so far and fast by waiting for things to happen.

"Very well, make ready to scout for a subspace conduit. We shall proceed toward the Alastic impoundment on Twelve... well within allied boundaries. That will leave us partially assisted by the Alastic far-sweep screens; if there are any de-cloaking warships out there, the screens will light 'em up. We can eavesdrop the screens while searching for holes. We shall have minimal exposure and maximum search time."

The group got up to leave; Ted Morgan interrupted.
"Oh, Carol... might I have a word, please?"
"Aye, sir"
She sat down; having a good idea what the word would be about. No doubt Majesty's sensor array picked up her pineal biorads when she was on Ala Nine.

Since erotic thoughts were strictly forbidden, and had been so for two centuries, the private convo had to be about her feelings. Sexual imagery had been taboo for so long that the entire officers' population felt highly uncomfortable even talking about it. If it were anyone but the Commander asking, Carol Three Feathers would report them to IG Fed just for asking. He sat back down, but this time, very close to her.
"Computer, two Probian ales, room temperature, snifter glasses, please."

"Aye, sir, two Probian ales, with worms."

Seconds later two beers appeared in the repro station, in over-size Probian bowls.

Morgan got up, took both and handed one to Three Feathers. They toasted at the same time.

"Eshtoika mahk."

"Carol, there were some rather unusual... fluctuations in the biorad scans when your away team was on... or rather, in... *the lake*. I am aware that the carbon dust, as well as Ala Nine's surface dust, can adversely affect Majesty's sensor function."

He drew a breath, preparing to enter the unspeakable realm of passion and lust.

"Now, it wasn't just your biorad that glitched... every team member had a, uh... similar glitch."

Carol's face blushed in confirmation and her eyes dropped to study the bottom of her glass, feigning interest in the Probian worms eagerly emitting carbon dioxide to fizzle the thick red ale. Morgan always left his officers some outs, and this subject definitely called for good ones.

"So the sensors were probably mis-reading due to carbon artifact... and... "

Just then, Morgan paused the talk.

"Computer, enable highest security cloak; this conversation to be only available to Intergalactic Federation, High Counsul MAYDAY Com."

"One moment, Commander... aye, sir, alpha security cloak, IG Federation high commission, fatal inquest only. You are hi-cloak-enabled, sir."

To verify, Morgan tried it out.

"Computer, open file on current conversation;"

"Aye, sir... *no such conversation exists.*"

Good... Alpha high-lock was in place.

"Carol, we shall never again speak of this, but recent... *events* make it imperative that I ask you... and believe me, it is only for the safety of this vessel that I am now asking..."

She trembled and blushed; never had she been subjected to "Top-Lock" convo; it was normally reserved only for courts martial.

"Aye sir, ask away."

"I couldn't help but notice it, this... well, I'll just go ahead and say it... this 'arousal' biorad, which every away team member displayed at the same time. Tutok's cortex even emitted arousal biorad, and for a Tahetan, that's an extremely difficult emotion to provoke... so clearly, some outside force... or forces must have been at work on my away team. I need to know what those forces were, for the ship's safety."

It seemed so surreal, sitting with the Commander, drinking contraband ale and discussing the most taboo subject... and yet he had a great way of putting distance between her passion and a full-staff capital tribunal.

"Yes sir, outside forces, aye sir."

He eyed his security officer intently for deception, already knowing he wouldn't find any; Three Feathers would die before she'd lie.

"Well, I commend you for your honesty, Carol... but now I must force the point, and for that I apologize; some of my duties are distasteful, and none more than this... But I need to know; how did it feel when you were standing in... *water?*"

Actually, he knew about wild water, but he used it for a scapegoat to help his officer. She had her out, and eagerly jumped at it.

"Oh, Commander, it was... indescribable; you should've been there! The scent of wild, free water... it was so exhilarating! We all felt it! The next thing I knew, we were all stripping off our suits. The marines, sir, their... what's that ancient term... their penises... raised to fully functional status, sir. They were..."

"You didn't ...?"

"No sir, I did not engage, but I must admit I had a burning desire to do that..."

"That's all right, Carol... we're only human."

His words were too dismissive, too small to describe such profound feelings; she felt the urge to purge, to somehow convey to him her passion.

"But sir, but that's not all. I watched them enter the water... four nude muscular bodies... my body felt a heat like no other. My eyesight turned red with... *passion*. I'm so sorry, sir. I'll try to never let it happen again... but the feeling of that water up to my waist? I'll remember it always. I felt free, like I had no duties or boundaries or consequence; for a moment I had a drive to copulate... with all of them... *even Tutok!*"

He thought and drank half his ale in silence; here was his top security officer, confessing to the unspeakable crime of passion. It ruined ships in the old days, this damned passion... and so it had first been outlawed, drugged and surgically, then later genetically, removed from all IG Fed staff and crew members.

And now his best security officer admitted to outright passion; not some vestigial blush, but full-heat, Pineal gland erectile, urges to copulate with every nude man in the lake.
It shocked the man who'd seen most of what the universe had to offer in the way of shocking stuff.

He needed to give her another out; wracking his brain, he found it by giving her an ally. It was a big sacrifice, but he didn't want to lose her.

"Perhaps there is some invisible force at work here, something affecting us all. It has happened to other crews at other places."

"Aye, sir, perhaps something like that."

Meanwhile, Three Feathers secretly wondered why she alone was being interrogated; after all, the marines were also in full lust mode... and probably Tutok also. Those Tahetans were so tough to read.

"Well, Carol Three Feathers, last of the Cherokee blood line, I salute your honest, forthright spirit; we've seen combat and way too many Hawk speeds together to hoard secrets! It's time I shared something with you, too."

He drained his ale and swallowed the undulating glow-green fermenting worms. They bit his tongue and throat defensively, all the way down. Twin trickles of warm blood leaked down his throat, spicing the ale further.

"Ah... nothing like a Probian ale to loosen the tongue; and so I must know tell you... I once experienced the same... *passion.*"

She went numb with his confession.

"Sir I shouldn't... I don't thi..."

"No, I'm telling you this because I know what you went through... You see, I took a sniff of the flower, and then I had these incredible feelings of lust and passion. Then I was surprised to find they lasted far longer than I thought... It stirred up old feelings, the likes of which I haven't felt since before I was taken into IG Fed's fold."

He smiled briefly.

"To be truthful... *it felt great.*"

She squirmed in her seat, and not from the worms biting her tongue, either. Nobody wanted a commander to out himself so completely...

But he was on a roll.

"You're the best security officer I've ever had, and I refuse to lose you because of some outside, uncontrollable force. I am writing this entire thing off as a sensor disturbance caused by carbon dust contamination. We'll speak no more of this... Fair?"

"Aye, sir; very fair, sir. Thank you!"

Again she felt passion, but this time it was for the job that she loved. They exited the room and hit the bridge. She put it behind her, but Morgan had trouble trying to put it out of his mind... standing in wild water; what he wouldn't give, to have that sensation again. He cursed those Federation rules about commanders staying on the ship... What a bunch of IK-Tah.

Harder stood over the helmsman's shoulder, peering into the sensor panels. By crossing the phasers and side scanners, it was possible to find the outline of a subspace conduit; when the scan beam and phaser beam collided, the resulting EMR burst would instantly energize a small piece of space.

Then in four milliseconds, the scorching rays dissipated, leaving any such holes temporarily outlined in phosphorescence from space debris. As the space dust particles' outer shell electrons resumed their normal orbital shells, they gave off a signal; for a split second, the rim would glow. As there was no other way to spot the outline, human eyes were needed.

First Officer Harder was first to stare into the blank recesses of space; the optical equivalent to spotting a single fish splashing in an ocean of choppy blue whitecaps on a windy day.

It was a tough task, so Harder took it first; he preferred to lead by example. Or so he told himself, but to spot an SSC meant immortality. One got to name it and forever after, every galactic mariner would know the conduit by that name. Will Harder was hopeful; he already had a name picked out for it.

He used to read ancient historical bubble chips about Pre-Blast Earth; one hobby they had was called; 'fishing,' which apparently had to do with pulling cold-blooded vertebrates from bodies of wild water. He vowed to go fishing if the chance ever presented. Since he hadn't yet seen wild water, the mythical concept of fishing held his fascination. And, since finding a conduit also bordered on the mythical, his christening term would be *"The Fishing Hole."*

Four hours later, Harder's eyes were shot. Reluctantly he gave the post over to Tutok, whose power of optical concentration was legendary. Coupled with his awesome mind, Tahet Tutok had something earthlings didn't yet have; every Tahetan had four eyes at birth or else they were killed immediately. And, just as others of his race, Tutok had the capacity to look in four directions at once, and to discern all four images, making him a great choice for such demanding optical work.

Officer Tutok became bored immediately with the snail's pace that Harder had ordered up, so he asked the Ensign to bring the Majesty up to Warp One... roughly forty times faster than Harder's previous search speed.

It was nine hours and forty-eight light years later when Tutok hit pay dirt.

"Ensign, please slow to half impulse."

"Aye, sir... one-half imp, aye."

Commander Morgan and the entire bridge sensed the decel and beamed straight to the bridge, eager to see a new thing; there on the lower left of the monitor was the mother of all conduits, its image frozen on the all-black screen. The outline appeared in phosphor-glow, a bluish tinged edge with a dim, purple core.

Commander Morgan was first to exit the reverie; "Well done, Tahet... *WELL DONE INDEED!*"
He pushed the ship's touch pad, putting it on all screens and holograph pods simultaneously.

"Attention all officers and crew. We are witnessing an historic event... Senior Science Officer Tahet Tutok has found an uncharted Subspace Conduit!"

Morgan waited for all hands to quit cheering, so his message would get through.

"We will have an official christening ten hours from now; all available hands are invited. But for now... drinks are on the house!" Then he realized that most of his crew had no access to ancient pre-blast earth colloquialisms; having lost all meaning four hundred years ago.

"That means I'm buying all drinks at Liberty Bay, Discovery Bay, Victory Bay and Down Under... And, when you lift your glass, toast the finest science officer in the Federation; that's an order!"

The crew was jubilant while senior staff just stood there, mesmerized. Rija spoke first.

"Will you look at the *SIZE* of it... you could float two starships wide through that maw!"

It was true enough; the Tutok Conduit, if that's what they would christen it, was larger than any known SSC. And to make it even better, it was practically a stone's throw from Ala Nine. Even a slow freighter could get to it in about forty hours. However, Tutok quickly tempered the staff's budding enthusiasm.

"Sir, permission to deploy a boomerang buoy to ascertain the conduit's destination and safety?"

"Granted, of course!"

Morgan was practically giddy; his name would go down in the annals of space mariners. Of his many achievements, this had to be the biggest. He pressed his throat pad.

"Attention Cargo Bay 24... Rig one boomerang buoy. Notify me when it is ready to deploy."

"One boomer, aye, sir, right away."

The buoy was ready in thirty minutes, after the crew loaded it with all the requisite claim data; ship and commander's names, star date, solar date, star-chart coordinates and of course, IG Federation commissar numbers.

And, since conduits were notorious for having surprisingly diverse endpoints, it paid to be multi-lingual, hence the need for the lengthy download, including every major Hawk-capable society's language. It wouldn't do to have it found by someone who couldn't log the other end.

With the Majesty's fastest lingo computers, it still took twenty minutes to input slightly less than forty-eight trillion languages. Then just to be sure, the crew copied boomer One into Boomer Two, in case Boomer One fell into unreliable hands or was lost to the vagaries of subspace conduit exploration.

Everyone who'd ever spent a semester in college knew that SSC endpoints wiggled around a little; on average, a radius of approximately five light years. But since they offered such monumental savings in time, shipping costs and resources, chasing a whipping end port for a few hours was well worth it.

The cargo bay crew sounded excited.

"Commander, Boomer One ready, sir."

"Stand by, Cargo Bay"

"Aye, Sir!"

Although excited, Ted Morgan knew he might forget something vital to this historic event.

"Officer Tutok, what are we missing?"

"Sir, if protocols are to be followed, I believe a scorching flare should go first."

"Of course, you're right... it's not every day we get to dedicate a conduit!"

He tapped the com pad.

"Cargo Bay 24, prepare a scorching flare with twin perpendicular phaserite-lenses. Rig it with double Cesium/tritium gel packs, maximum voltage and duration. I don't want it fizzling before we find the other end."

"Aye, sir, double hot-pencils, four trillion mega-joules... it'll scorch for ten EASY sir, unless someone shuts it off."

"Outstanding! Inform me when scorcher's ready."

"Aye, sir."

He eyed Tutok for approval, but he was way ahead of him.

"Sir, it is widely accepted that the size of the openings are proportional to their lengths; with the singular exception of the Rogers Conduit, near Core Space... This conduit could be the longest yet, sir."

"Outstanding!"

"Aye, sir, but we know some of the longer conduits have Nidus formations and Schmorl's leaks; I recommend spinning the scorching flare at high rate, to mark any bulges, leaks or rifts."

Ted Morgan got the idea fast. It wouldn't do to lose the buoy to some vagrant solar breeze blasting through a Nidus or having the buoy take a wrong turn down a Schmorl... he would be the laughing stock of the charted galaxies.

"Very well, Tutok... an excellent point!"

With a light heart he tapped the com pad.

"Cargo, rig scorcher for maximum spin; set it to start one second before lock-on."

"Aye, sir; rigging for six thousand revs, spin the top before lock... we'll have it ready shortly, sir."

That was all they could do to secure the hole for the Intergalactic Federation; scorch it, probe it, claim it. Finding any SSC was historic enough. Very few tunnels ever did open up somewhere near useable space... but if this one did, it would be a treasure of monumental proportions. Everyone on board would be known throughout the galaxies; wherever they might go, drinks would be on the house, just because they were aboard the Majesty when she found the tunnel. The Cargo crew hustled to rig the flare.

"Cargo Bay 24 to bridge; scorching flare is ready."

"Very well, set PDI coordinates for the aperture's center and ship it."

"Aye, sir. Already set; firing now."

In four seconds the bridge crew saw the tiny flare materialize, spinning rapidly near the mammoth opening; its extreme spin rate made it look like a solid light, at the center of occasional scorching bits of space dust and micrometeors.

The flare entered the aperture, leaving in its wake just a tiny glowing trail of scorching, phosphorescing space debris to mark its trajectory. Tutok made an involuntary noise when he saw the trail of glowing beads. For Tutok, that was most unusual.

Morgan touched the compad.
"Very good! The scorcher's in the hole. Deploy Boomerang Buoy."
"Aye, sir; boomer away and tracking scorch points."
"Outstanding!"

All eyes again went to the monitor, surprised to see the boomerang traveling so much slower. Obediently logging and homing the center of the flare path, Boomer One traveled at half the speed of the scorcher.
Tutok had time to verify that the language tongues and all IG Fed patent codes were fully operational in hail mode before releasing the

electromagnetic tether, and then the boomer disappeared into the hole.

The senior staff stood there, awed at the significance; they had just found the first subspace conduit in twenty-five EASY. Beyond that, it was likely to be the longest conduit of all.

All that remained was to await the boomer's return, download its star chart data and record the position of the other end.

But of them all, only Ensign El-Tar Bok-Tah, from the planetary system Poov-Ran, felt no such awe. Perhaps his youth prevented him from being aware of the magnitude of the moment. But more likely it was his annoying pragmatism. He was always the one who loved to point out the "what if" scenario. This conduit posed several. If there was one major problem, it had to be with the terminus; it could end up in some deserted sector where it served no purpose.

Then their discovery, while still an historic event, wouldn't mean much to IG Fed; if they couldn't ship cargo through it, what use was it? Worse yet, it might terminate near Borg Space or worse than that, the Territories Klog... in which case it could give their greatest archenemies instant access to plenty of vulnerable civilizations without time to evacuate their home systems.

He shuddered to think of the deadliest and most merciless killers in all the charted galaxies; Klog Death Cubes. Wherever they traveled, every living thing perished. Up until now, the only way to escape the Klog was speed, since the Death Cubes were slower than Pre-blast tortoises. When it came to velocity, their technology lapsed several centuries behind; the Klog cared for killing, not for speed. But if the Klog should somehow stumble upon subspace conduits, the resulting annihilation would be unimaginable.

El-Tar knew conduits only from his studies at IG Fed Officers' school. Finally he could contain his concerns no longer.

"Sir, what if this conduit ends up useless to commerce?"

Tutok, slightly annoyed at the skinny little buzz killer, answered.

"Ensign, we log what we see... the useless and the useful. At some point, perhaps the useless becomes significant. But should this conduit terminate in desolate space, we can still explore it. Sometimes another aperture can be found near the termination aperture... If we find another, then we can essentially leapfrog from one to the next, saving decades of space-sleep travel. Would that satisfy you?"

The young ensign blushed deeply at the Officer's quasi-sarcastic reprimand. He wasn't supposed to blush, but then again, he wasn't supposed to ask stupid questions, either.

Just then the boomerang popped back out of the aperture. The crew was fairly surprised.
 "Number One, tractor beam the buoy within 100 kilometers and perform routine evocon and software security scans"
"Aye, sir."

The crew stood immobilized, awaiting the data. It was a long three minutes until Will nodded.

"Sir, all systems appear to be normal. No virus, no comp-jackers and definitely no hostiles have interacted with the buoy, sir."

Morgan smiled deeply.

"Outstanding! Bring her aboard so we can see where she's traveled."

"Aye, sir; to Engineering Deck Two."

Whenever massive computing tasks were needed, Majesty's Deck Two fit the bill. For calculating Hawk travel routes or charting galaxies, it was almost perfect, except for the lack of a proper universal data cross-port. Fortunately, Under-Captain Rob was the perfect tool for the interaction between boomerang and ship's engineering computers.

They up-linked the boomer, plugging into Rob's CGI cross-port, just to be sure they wouldn't contaminate Majesty's star chart database. If any viruses or cybergnomic transclones got inside the boomer, Rob would die first, before Majesty was threatened.

It was no small risk, either; Rob was relatively unique... To replace him would cost the Federation dearly; there were only three Robs in the entire IG Fed command. Still, better to risk a robodroid than Majesty herself.

Rob twitched when the boomer began downloading its incredible volume of travel data and constellation photos. His eyes closed. His tempoparietal fins emerged. Rob's cybercortical turbocoolers turned on, a sign of massive overheating. The fins, in spite of the turbocooling, turned dull red. Then suddenly they cooled, the coolers turned off and Rob recovered.

"Commander, the data is uncontaminated, but is quite extensive. I recommend disengaging me, to speed up transfer rates or it could take several years, sir."

Morgan and Tutok both knew this meant a shitload of data, because Rob's neural net never slowed down during a transfer before.

"Very well, Rob, disengage. Put transfer on the screen, please."

"Aye, sir."

The huge comp screen became a blur of star panels, each changing so fast that the naked human eye couldn't register the sight. Even Tutok's unique optical processing speeds could not keep up with the sequential blinks.

"Unbelievable!"

Tutok, not given to such hyperbole, was nonetheless correct. The new conduit was extremely long, incredibly smooth and free from Schmorl's herniations, Nidus formations and other anomalies, as far as they could tell.

Five minutes later, the fireworks display ended. A single star panel remained; clearly the last place visited by the boomerang. Rob spoke first.

"Commander, that last panel looks familiar, but impossible... scanning my charts; Commander, I believe... Yes, definitely... Sir, it is the *Nexion Configuration."*

Now it was Tutok's turn to swear.

"Qurt Fak... sorry sir, I meant to..."

"Never mind, Tutok, a Tahetan curse word certainly is called for! Allow me a similar, an old one from Pre-blast English; *FUCK ME!* We couldn't be luckier if we'd carved the tunnel ourselves!"

It wasn't the time or place for Tutok to correct the Commander on his linguistical error; Qurt Fak literally translated as *"Impossible"*, which, to the science-minded Tahetans, was the mother of all curse-words.

Ensign El-Tar Bok-Tah obviously didn't share their enthusiasm; Ship's Gunner Patel tried to explain the significance to the young bookworm.

"The terminus lies in the far corner of the Nexion, which is just a hundred million light years from IG Fed Central, and only 8 Million from Earth! Imagine! A split-second in the tunnel and we'd be out; even at Warp speeds, we could be on Earth in just a couple days!"

The Commander wanted to stop all talk of going to Earth or to any other "home" planet within a million light years of the terminus.

"More to the Federation's interests, *a CARGO SHIP,* even a junk freighter full of Heavy-tritium crystal, could easily make Earth in six weeks.... Maybe a month, with sufficient solar sails! Can you imagine the savings to the Federation? Most freighters can do six weeks without even going to vac-dried food!"

Tutok did the rough math; "Assuming typical freighter loads from Ala Nine at customary freighter velocities, say... Warp four to the aperture, all-stop in the tunnel and exit at Warp Five to Federation labs on ALK-TAS SIX... in four point five weeks; assuming present terminus positions, sir."

Morgan whistled softly. He hadn't dreamed of such savings.

"Sire of God! We'll save freighter crews six EASY of space sleep per trip! Think of it; no step-downs, no DNA scrubs and no decel packing! Add that comfort to the savings... it's unbelievable! I must notify the full crew!"

He touched the com pad.

"Commander to the entire crew... The SSC extends almost to Earth's doorstep; and it appears to have no anomalies! We shall christen in six hours! Prepare for a celebration! That is all."

He sat back and sighed, as content as a Commander can afford to get. Three Feathers brought him back to reality.

"Sir, I suggest we drop the SSC search and re-energize our cloak scanners?"

"Certainly; make it so."

She sighed with relief; flying through space with their pants down was pure torture for the security specialist; it left her feeling more naked than bathing with those Marines. Fifty seconds later, all systems normal, she was relieved to see no evidence of Carnelians, Lividians or other sneaky bastards out there in the shadows.

Ted Morgan stood up to leave the bridge.

"Well, it has been a great day indeed... Number One, you have the con. I'm getting some rest."

"Aye, sir. I have the con; sweet dreams."

The-soon-to-be-mythical hero headed for chambers to do some serious thinking.

FOUR...

KI

Captain Fooling Wee paused only briefly to hear about the SSC. He was a busy doctor, with little time for space politics, corporate savings or galactic turf wars; he hadn't yet heard of a conduit being used to save a single life... nor did he expect to.

Fooling was the finest doctor on Majesty. His credentials spanned decades and four specialties. Although physical diagnosis was a lost art, Fooling excelled in it. Not that he'd saved any human species yet with it, of course... the ship's genetic sensors did all that. But as for minority races around the galaxies, the ship's database was paltry. His knowledge of old-school physical saved many a life. One of his miracles even prevented a civil war on Galos Seven.

But so much for politics... Fooling loved healing things. His craving for knowledge and discovery was responsible for saving hundreds of plant, animal and viral species from certain extinction... and he accomplished it without sanction; quite an honor, considering IG Fed's Imperial Directive and their totalitarian clamp on interference of any kind.

That was why he'd applied for residency on Majesty; she had a history of sailing into uncharted space, and discovery knows no better workbench than naked, raw space.

When Fooling wasn't studying or healing things, he was in the display labs. The nearly endless rows of artifacts, specimens and living organisms required constant doting. Doctor and Surgeon Fooling Wee was perfect for the job.

His latest subject was the thorn-less rose, recently taken from Ala Sphenoidis Nine. It was a quizzical entity, this rose, if one could call it that. It was more rose than lily, and it had no thorns.

At Fooling's side was his Number Two assistant, Chastity Basil Thorngood; an overly plump female from Post-Blast Earth's New Synthetic London. This was her second voyage on Majesty... to say she was curious would be a huge understatement.

"Oh, Doctor; it's so beautiful... have you ever seen such a pretty rose?"

"I don't think I have, Chastity, but it's most unusual for several reasons."

"Do you mean the lack of thorns?"

Fooling went into his professor mode, talking down to subordinates; a role he thoroughly enjoyed.

"Yes, its stalk resembles that of the Lion-Killer Lilly I named and studied on Ugumbu's fourth wet planet, near the Criterion Nebula, in Sargassian Space. And what an experience that was!"

The very thought made his skin burn from those damnable fire-chiggers.

"The lion-killer lily waits for the spring rains to puddle. Then in a botanical miracle, it grows three feet tall, in a single night.

She gasped; *"Really?"*

"Before dawn, the lily will bud, spread its petals and spew its odors to the winds... it smells exactly like a pregnant Govorkian cow's placental blood. Any nearby lions come quickly, hoping for an easy calf-kill. When the lion comes, it sniffs the lily, which spews a highly concentrated form of Curare; within seconds, the lion falls, and death follows in minutes."

"Oh, how... horrible."

Wee knew only three things about the universe, after wandering in it for decades. He liked to call them "Fooling's Triad."

Nothing is free.

There is no good or bad.

There is only what is.

"Chastity, one deed always sets another into motion. The lion killer lily can't eat a whole lion, But the hyena-like Durango Dogs love lion flesh. They can find a dead lion within half an hour.

The Durango always urinates and defecates when it finds a kill, to mark it... and that benefits the lily."

"Within the Durango intestine resides a special type of platyhelminth. When it is passed to the ground, the flat worm burrows and lays several million offspring. The lily roots picks up the nymphals. They work their way to the plant's core before releasing their fissionary byproducts, which is what the lily needs to produce lure scent, curare and pollen."

She nodded enthusiastically.

"Ah; a complex cycle."

"Soon after the pollen granules appear, the flat worms also mature. Scavenger flies pollinate the lily; the worms hitchhike on the flies, waiting to be deposited on the eyelids of sleeping lions. Migrating Govorkian cows eat the lily; petals, stalk and all... ingesting the worms also."

"Yes?"

"So the lily kills the lion that ate the cow that ate the flower that killed the lion... and the worms benefit from each step in the transaction. One of the universal laws remains intact. I call it Fooling's Imperative...

> Everything goes to the worms,
> sooner or later."

His assistant went silent. Actually, she knew all about cycles of life, but a little ass kissing goes a long way. She knew when to quit.

Fooling Wee again eyed the strange new rose and pondered what hidden cycles it must participate in... Perhaps as the ancient Pre-Blast Earth playwright said, a rose is just a rose... but Shakespeare was dead... *LONG dead*.

Ordinarily, such a specimen aroused suspicion and caution in any scientist of his stature. But all predator plants he'd ever studied showed big red flags during initial evo-con scans.

Majesty showed that the scan on this one was perfect; although the first scan showed some sort of vanishing ghost image. But after re-calibration, subsequent scans showed the normal Uridian

Systems DNA double helix, which comprised the bulk of this particular galaxy layer of life.

Each race had its own name for it. On Pre-Blast Earth they used to call it "Watson/Crook's Double Helix". Way over in Tessla's Universe it was called "Spiral of Life." On Taurus Five it was Budding's Twisted Ladder, and on the Julca systems, Ki, meaning "life stuff". The Julcans were so efficient in their simplicity.

But after the IG Feds aggressively established their inter-galactic scientific nomenclature system, DNA's newest term became "evo-con," meaning evolutionary-conscriptive ingredients.

Still, Fooling preferred the ancient earth term, DNA. So inside his lab, that's what he called it. But for his obligatory periodic subspace waveform reports, he always deferred to IGASL nomenclature. He didn't want anyone from the International Galactic Applied Science Linguistics busting his chops. Those paper pushers were such relentless assholes.

So the rose's DNA was found to be good. But beyond the tangible printouts, the rose emitted something much less tangible. It puzzled the doctor. It seemed that it lost its luster when alone, but when visitors gathered to admire the beautiful plant, it seemed to perk up. It was most puzzling.

FIVE...
CHRISTENING

The entire crew of Majesty watched wall panels, holograph pods and cocktail monitors in each of the ship's four lounges. As for Majesty, she sat at all stop with minimal security crew on duty, just four million kilometers from the soon-to-be-christened subspace conduit.

The entire crew celebrated with the honorary drink; Pilk-Rah, Tahet Tutok's drink of choice from his native planet. The English translation; "Island Joy," a fermented berry juice with plenty of alcohol, thanks to Tahet's special fermenting bacteria, which easily tolerated alcohol levels as high as 24 percent before dying off. It kicked like a mule, but as it was Tutok's moment, and to drink anything else would dishonor him.

Soon the Commander occupied the holograph pods and screens. He planned to be brief.

"On this historic occasion, I would first thank the crew for its outstanding performance and commitment to Majesty and her goals. It is to that loyalty, epitomized by Master Science Officer Tutok, that we are gathered. He spotted this Subspace Conduit, and in accordance with Intergalactic Federation law, has the right to christen it. But for the record, I shall first qualify his name, rank and position..."

"Officer Tutok is Master Science Officer aboard this vessel, IG Federation Starship Majesty, Sailing Number Zero Six One."

"He is originally from the planet Tutok, sixth planet orbiting Dar Ok, a middle class White-star in Stratos Seven of the Uridian Galaxy, star chart 0912, SS 7, Coordinate grid code 564-7, dot Urid."

"Officer Tahet Tutok's professional achievements justify his christening honors; they are legendary within the Uridian Layers of galaxies and even further into the cosmos."

"He graduated Tahet University with double Masters' in Photoneuroimmunology and Liquid Transphysical Calculus, at the age of twelve. From there, Tutok interned at the Galos teaching facility in Bethels Colony Four, earning Ship's Master in Science and Intergalactic Linguistic Protocol, with Honors."

The commander took a sip to wet his lips.

"At age fifteen, he became the only ILP Master to ever be recruited by the Intergalactic Federation. By age nineteen, Master Tutok developed the prototype for the UNBP, commonly known as the Universal Neurolinguistic Business Port... something every space mariner now takes for granted. For that, he received the galaxy's highest award in Science and Engineering, Darwin's Feather. Every time you plug a translation hypercrystal into your Trifacial Nerve-port, you have Master Tahet Tutok to thank, for without it, we would all be essentially blind to transphysical database cross-loading. Interspace communication would slow to a crawl, were it not for Tutok's Port."

The ship's crew vibrated Majesty's hull with roars of approval, forcing a pause in the narrative of accolades. Without Tutok's throat port, they couldn't even curse in an alien language, much less get any work done.

Commander Morgan took a big breath.

"Master Tutok then became the youngest senior officer on this very vessel, Majesty, the finest in the known galaxies!"

Now the hull roared, com channels hummed and drinks flowed. Even those who disliked Tutok's cold personality had to bow in homage to his legendary achievements.

"I am honored to have Tahet Tutok as an outstanding Science Officer and good friend... Ladies and gentlemen, officers and crew, and of course all who shall see this event on inter-space bubble chips, subspace broadcast, empathic envoy or wave-quark recorders, I give you, with great pleasure, Science Officer Tahet Tutok..."

The ship went crazy with applause, dying only when Tutok's mouth opened to speak.

"Thank you, Commander Morgan. I am honored to have such kind words spoken. But these achievement is the byproduct of what has been achieved before. To see further, one must stand upon the shoulders of willing and able peers. I have had excellent shoulders to stand upon."
He cleared his throat.
"I have given thought to christening this new Subspace Conduit. Although Federation rules can be lifted for naming it after Majesty or myself, there is one among us that I have admired."

The crew buzzed, for nobody ever noticed Tutok admiring anything but positron microscopes and trans-dimensional spectrophotometers.

"Her courage and sense of duty is exemplary... as with all of Majesty's crew. But there is more than courage and loyalty that sets Security Officer Carol Three Feathers apart."

The crew buzzed at the name.

"Long ago, far away on Uridian System's Pre-Blast Earth, a primitive race of fierce warriors lived. They were a proud people, honoring truth and courage and all other concepts that the universe holds true. Then the invaders came. They brought superior weapons and soon dominated the Cherokee Nation. They took their land; there was no Imperial Directive back then."

The crew went silent to think of such anarchy.

"The Cherokee were forced to walk thousands of kilometers from their homeland, forced to live a subservient life of dishonor and poverty in a strange and horrible land not suited to the Cherokee people. Many died on this trail. Their families kept walking while they cried in grief... Soon it was called the "Trail of Tears.""

"When our scorching beacon first made for the conduit, it lit up thousands of phosphorescing bits of space debris, and the sight triggered my memory of those archival history lessons of Pre-Blast Earth and the Cherokee Nation's plight."

"The conduit's opposing terminus lies in the far corner of the Nexion, approximately 8 Million light years from Earth. It must have been visible on primitive earth at orbital equinoxes, back before Hawkins Travel contaminated space light and obliterated low-intensity star sparkle. It would have showed as a dim glow during crepuscular times, given sufficient aurora. Perhaps that is what the Cherokee Nation prayed to as their Great Spirit.

"When the Cherokee were forced off their land, they did not do well. Within 600 solar orbits, nothing remained of the race, save for a few curios and artifacts. Then the small wet-planet banged from intercontinental thermonuclear war. After recovery, approximately 400 solar orbits later, genome tracers located several hairs, whose indigenous, native evolutionary-conscriptive ingredients were as yet un-logged.

"They re-hydrated the ancient evo-con. Soon a dark young native homo sapiens bipedal male emerged... a Cherokee warrior."

The crew kept silent at the concept.

"But the male was too high spirited, too... unfit for conventional purposes, so he was terminated, his Qui-Gong and evo-con logged and cryo-stored."

"Later, when IG-Fed came to power, emphasis was placed upon re-stirring vestigial native Uridian systems evo-con, because it was getting too stratified from excessive cloning. When they replicated the Cherokee strain, they only made one test Cherokee... Officer Carol Three Feathers, one of the finest officers with which I have had the pleasure to work."

The crew applauded.

"I would honor her race and symbolize the terminus... To those who died so long ago on the Trail of Tears, while looking to the heavens for help I christen; The Great Spirit Conduit. Good bye."

Tutok simply turned and went back to his workstation. Morgan again took the podium.

"Very good, Tahet Tutok, very good... *The Great Spirit Conduit* it is! Computer, make the proper logs and send off a moniker buoy to IG Federation."

"Aye, buoy away, sir... and... congratulations."

After that, crew-members that weren't too drunk went back to work. The rest kept the party going until lights out.

Inside the science lab, Fooling and staff partied hard; it had been a great voyage for science... first the two new species; a Fire Frog from Dalcon Eight, then the rose and now this new SSC. It was a scientist's Mother Lode.

Wee and his five understudies gathered round the rose, but now they were drinking synthetic hooch of their own making. Weaker than the Tahetan drink but far tastier, they had a good buzz going, and tomorrow was a pure-travel day... they could sleep in.

The party soon gathered around the flower, which seemed more vibrant than ever. Dr. Fooling Wee, being an a-sex, didn't feel its sexual effects. Nor was he sober enough to observe the effects upon his staff. They brushed hips.

Vestiges of long-dormant sexual drives began stirring. The two clones, Kate Four and Five, began to show anterior cervical flushing... most atypical, for clones. Along with the Kates, Susan Willows began to feel hot. Taft and Burroughs, both original-sex remnant-males, were likewise drugged into criminal arousal status... and just like the women, they weren't aware of their crime; just like the away team on Ala Nine.

Before long they swayed like one organism, dancing to the tune of the plant... its pheromones working on the foolish primates. Luckily for Majesty, there weren't enough targets present to trigger, so the rose just stayed shut, content to spew 'come get me' drugs into the air. And from there? Into the ship's HVAC ducts, of course. The effect spread to several cubic kilometers of Majesty's internal space... mostly to science and engineering levels. Some crewmembers hid their partial erections, fearing loss of their job if anyone saw them.

Two fistfights broke out, even though fistfights had been banned for two centuries. They were crude and poorly executed, but they were still fistfights. One female originally from Aphoria Seven, where sexual activity had only recently been banned, noticed lactation; one single wet drop at each nipple. Not knowing what it was, she beamed straight to sickbay.

Fortunately the science party ended; Wee passed out on the lab floor, under the rose display. Both Kates and Willows made it to their berths. Taft and Burroughs crapped out near the gilled fire frog tank. Just before they fell asleep they were sad the girls were gone. Sadness, of all things, imagine that! Nobody felt sadness any more.

But of them all, the rose was the saddest. Had there been fifty more primates surrounding her, she would have killed them all. The rose grew a small clone. And then it grew two more. Were it not for a paucity of hydroponics feed, it would have spawned two thousand death roses right then and there.

SIX...

CLONES

Morgan awoke to doorbell chimes; "Enter."

Fooling Wee entered without his customary deferential bow; so excited he forgot protocol.

"Commander... look at *THIS!*"

"Yes, it's beautiful... *So what?*"

In his arms were the rose, specimen tray and all; "Sir, last night after the party, it was just one... now it's FOUR. *Don't you see?*"

Still nursing a hangover from the Tahetan swill, Ted was impatient.

"Come to the point"

"Sir, for a plant, it's fairly anomalous to sprout and grow three more, almost to maturity in just a few hours."

"SO?"

"Commander, we can send one with the emissary shuttle... straight to IG Fed's Halcyon, sir. We'll have enough for study, and Hal can genotype it *without us having to head home, sir.*"

"Very well! Make it so. And now that we have four, leave one here with me. Thank you, Fooling. That is all."

The doctor left, dismayed at the chief's lack of enthusiasm. For a Commander with such incredible leadership talent, he sure didn't care shit about plants. Wee thought about kicking his ass. Then he started walking and the pheromones couldn't keep up with him. The violent thoughts quickly faded in the fresh air.

The Commander had some nasty thoughts, too, but they evaporated when his thin wire brought out the opiates. In ten seconds, Morgan was too high to give HELL a fuck about anything.

The plant's lure hit Sick Bay, too. Zoe Paktah, originally from Aphoria Seven in the Trident Nebula System, hailed a male nurse.

"Hey Kent, look at my chest!"

He eyed the woman's chest quizzically for a second before realizing her copolymer leotard had dual concentric wet spots... a medical oddity he had never seen.

"What are those?"

He touched the wet spots and she jumped backward... but not before unexpected electric tingles pulsed through her body. It felt weird, scary and... good.

He smelled his finger, then tasted the liquid and immediately felt his loins stirring.

"Oh, sorry, Zoe... but it appears to be an... exudate... of some kind. I'll call the surgeon!"

Just then the sick bay quarantine vents came on and blew the pheromones away from them. Their heads cleared. By the time they met the ship's surgeon, Zoe's nipples were back to their flat, inert state of normalcy.

SEVEN...
TRAVELS

Carnassian Underlord Dahk Tah hissed into the ship's com system for all to hear.

"Gods-be-damned... I will buy all hands a barrel of Pintos-Pure when we can get off this Dalerian Pig and get back in a *REAL FIGHTING SHIP!*"

There were only four warriors aboard, but his offer was still sincere. They jumped into action to serve their underlord, whose name translated roughly into English as; 'Bringer of Death.' He hated the rusted, moldy Carnelian cargo ship. As far as freighters went, it was a real piece of space-cuke shit... it had no water except for one puny single-tap synthesizer in the tiny galley. It had poor fore and aft travel monitors, too... he could barely see through them.

He wondered how the Carnelians could even maneuver, much less carry cargo and repel pirates, with such miserable vessels. Inwardly however, he admired warriors who could achieve so much with such pathetic tools. No doubt that was why they had successfully repelled all prior attacks by his fellow Carnassians.

And, doubtlessly, they would still be repelling them if it hadn't been for the Death Rose. Admittedly, it was pure star-bat shit to resort to such cowardly ways to kill one's enemy. But they rationalized it; to get to the Federation they would first have to destroy the Carnelians. So their longtime foes and unwilling half-brothers of the same solar system became nothing more than a subspace speed bump.

The Carnassians first discovered the rose at the other end of their domain, approximately four quarks straight 'down'... for lack of a better term; zero apogee by anyone's standard six-dimensional nav system.

But if 'down' has no meaning in space, then neither does 'first discovery'. Le Clerc -Tah, Carnass' only statesman, habitually said;

"Nothing is new under the two suns."

So if it was true for the binary system holding planets Carnass and Carnel with just its two spinning midget-suns, it must certainly be true for the entire universe and its countless stars. The universe is bigger than first and last or up and down. Nobody discovers a thing for the first time; the thing was already there, for a long, long time.

The Carnassians encountered the rose on a beautiful old planet with plenty of water, yet paradoxically no vertebrate life. The flower gave off a wonderful scent, so they were gathered and shipped home. Two unknown mineral samples also went, according to standard prospecting protocol. When the ship arrived at home orbit, all her non-Carnassian crewmembers were dead in their space-sleep pods.

Paradoxically, the Carnassian crewmembers arrived in excellent health.

They studied the roses, which numbered in the thousands after the short voyage. It didn't take long to find the flower's secrets. First were the attractive scents; universal pheromone lures and a fast-acting opiate compound. Incredibly, it gave a nice short term high without any visible side effects or crash later.

The other secret was its killing power. When sufficient numbers of prey species surrounded the rose, it would give off massive amounts of Carbon Dioxide, laced with short-acting sleep pheromones and a fast-acting form of aerial Digoxin; scans proved it was recently stolen from Ritnau-Six, but it was known only as Diek Pah to the Carnassians.

Invisible to most evo-con scans and ship-risk scans, Diek Pah stops most vertebrate species' hearts, then dissipates quickly. The drug combination proved highly effective; anyone falling asleep near the rose would quickly asphyxiate and/or die from Diek Pah. So they labeled their new super weapon; Urik -Tah... "The Death Rose."

Had it not been for the Carnassians' incredible ability to process massive quantities of Carbon Dioxide, they too would have perished.

But due to the extreme Carnassian planetary orbit anomalies, Carnass had long days; each day being equivalent to four Earth Atmosphere Standard-orbit Years.

Consequently, the thickly vegetated planet produced huge amounts of Oxygen during daylight and massive amounts of CO2 during the long nights. Over the millennia, the warrior race evolved a highly efficient pair of gills. One sat at either side of the larynx, wrapping around the neck, tapering to twin tails near the posterior midline. They gave the appearance of twin purple, horizontal, teardrops. With these highly specialized structures, the Carnassians actually thrived in low-ox, high CO2 atmospheres, where other species could not. The rose mission proved it. Being quick to see the military applications, the Carnassians rigged a trap for their enemies. They knew that Carnelians, with their rapid planetary spin rate and rare perpendicular orbit, had no such gills or any need for them, so the Death Rose ought to work great against them.

They sent out a cargo ship loaded with ortho-deuterium crystals and just one fighter escort. Such a sweet cheese was too much for the rats to resist. It took just one phaser blast of anionic cinch particles to kill the crew. They tractored the freighter home and promptly beamed down its addictive cargo to the center dock at AMIGDA-CARN... capital city of the planet.... Never had they had so much "Party Rock" in a single pile.

They partied all over the planet. Everyone got a hit of crystals... even the minors and drones got crystals. It was a hell of a party. When they came down from the drug, the whole planet was awash in beautiful red roses with no thorns, sweet scent and an intoxicating opiate residue.

Seeing the rose as a renewable resource for getting high, they spread them to the furthest sections of the planet. In less than a month, every land-based species on the planet was dead. All that remained were marine-based life forms and beautiful roses... and two feet of freshwater in her new lakes.

The Carnassians celebrated their victory for nearly a year... And then the great depression hit. As is so true with all military-driven economies, the Carnassians had been at war with the Carnelians for centuries. Their entire economy revolved around building weapons to kill and hospitals to heal their wounded. But once their Carnelians were gone, the economy plummeted. Without war, they had nothing. The entire solar system was theirs alone... and alone they were.

It took just a few pillaging treks to the deserted planet before they realized their folly. Carnel became just another empty planet. Its resources were similar to those on Carnass, so until they might need to evacuate to Carnel, they left it alone. The warriors found themselves, ironically, longing for their old enemy.

Still, the rose proved to be the greatest weapon of all. It killed off an entire race without costing anything more than two vessels and a small fortune in party crystals.

With nothing left to push against, a muscle becomes weak. So, too, the Carnassian war muscles were quickly weakening. They needed to find new enemies before their economy completely imploded. The next closest enemies lay fairly nearby, within the Ala Sphenoidis system. Convenient, that the last few surviving Carnelians were mining that very planet.

The Ala system held 24 useable planets. Each one held essentially the same resources; carbon fibers and frozen copolymer resin deposits... As per IG-Fed regs, various races were each allotted one carbon planet, beginning With Ala Three; the first two being too close to the sun for mining purposes. The claims were distributed in no particular order of significance, since all races were now supposedly considered equal.

There was but one mandatory condition; the race must be IG-Fed friendly for ten home system orbits, prior to staking claim.

And so the Carnelians, the latest race to comply with the IG Fed manifesto, won Ala Fourteen. That left Ala 15 through 24 unawarded... and conveniently enough, there were only seven hostiles left in nearby space.

So, there was ample bribe material left in the system; it would only be a matter of time before the few remaining pirate races tired of their pillaging ways and came into the flock. Or at least, that was the plan.

Putting the rose on Ala Fourteen was easy enough; the Carnassians lay cloaked on the dark side of the planet. When a freighter finally appeared and began beaming down supplies, the Carnassians simply infected the beam with rose clones. Six weeks later, every miner on Ala Fourteen was dead.

One thing dawned on the slow-thinking Carnassians while they waited for the miners to die; IG-Fed had cargo log sensors in stationary spatial grids to monitor shipping lanes. It wouldn't take a tactical genius to note the absence of Carnelian freighter travel. Suspicion would certainly follow. So the Carnassians occupied several dozen drifting Carnelian freighters. Odd that they never wondered why these freighters were out there, adrift. Had they known, they might have changed plans. The truth of it was, Carnelians already ferried the rose to other planets, bartering with other miners.

Regardless, the Carnassians sailed the freighters in the distribution lanes, triggering just enough grid sensors to allay IG Fed suspicion. They made a point to trigger only the remote sensors, which had no hull penetration technology. To these sensors, a ship was a ship... and cargo or lack of it be damned. On the other hand, proximity sensors for receiving planets were far smarter; they sensed not only full hulls; they could also spot viruses, evo-con hijackers, contraband and hazardous cargos.

EIGHT...

MINERS

The miners from all over Fourteen scurried to the loading docks on their scooters; most had ore wagons in E-Mag tow, anticipating plenty of food, smut chips and maybe some Ortho-Deuterium crystals. It didn't take much to keep them happy as long as they had party crystal and working neuro ports for the smut chips.

The miners loaded their wagons, pleased to see such beautiful roses... life on a desolate, carbon-black planet left much to be desired for scenery. Being highly sensitized to ortho-deuterium and other opiate derivatives, the Carnelian olfactory lobes easily sniffed the opiates inside the roses. They instantly nicknamed it the 'Glow-Rose.' They held high hopes for the Rose; if it worked, they wouldn't have to import O-D crystal.

The problem, though, was obvious; few Glow-Roses, many miners. Fights ensued and a few hundred shovel-phaser burns finally sorted it out. Holes Three and Fifteen took the five best roses. The last two flowers would stay on the loading dock for the time being; they would go to the teams that mined the most carbon fiber in one week; it was a race; a loaded race, but a race nonetheless.

Knowing that Three and Fifteen had the best ore veins and the strongest diggers, it was only a matter of time before those assholes would have all the pretty roses. This didn't sit well.

Perhaps it was the beam-down that triggered such rapid growth in the roses or maybe it was something else, something which only the Rose knew. But whatever it was, the plant kicked into its fastest clone mode. With almost a thousand primates surrounding them at holes 3 and 15, she put out lure scents to full capacity. Within three days the miners had four thousand clones;

they carried them to their hollows, down the shafts, even into the darkened smut chambers.

On the fourth night, just as Ala Fourteen's moons rose over the East wing, every rose simultaneously emitted its poison, snuffing life painlessly and silently. From the two best mines, there would be no miners coming to the race.

By race end, the two docked roses had also cloned enough for everybody, so the race results were moot. Nobody noticed that mines Three and Fifteen never showed up to claim their honors. Each mine got a few glow roses and everybody went back home.

It took just another week to kill them all. This left only one inhabitant on the planet. Old Gus Page had seen a lot of the universe. That wasn't his real name, because nobody could pronounce it... certainly not these dumb miners. He didn't give a care about pretty plants, and he sure didn't trust any species that just *appeared* in the wake of a beam-down. So he initially shied away from the thing. But now, with so many miners not coming back to the loading dock, he began to wonder about the flowers... they were everywhere.

And, with pheromones getting thicker than carbon dust, they saturated the atmosphere until the lure finally got to him. Gus started feeling wonderful, in spite of his rigid, drug-free Slipticklik upbringing. He brought one into his cubicle and studied it. When his miners came back, he'd have answers for them about this strange new flower.

The rose spewed opiates, but it grew confused at Gus Page's response; it was not typical for primates. Gus was unaffected... So the rose went to plan B... deep inside the stamen, she began to erect and telescope her third DNA stand.

The process took several minutes before the tri-fluted killer helix was fully erect and operational. Then another four minutes before there were sufficient tri-flutes to spare a few million killing spears. She tipped the spears with opiate-coated Corundum; sugar coated DNA strand-splitters of unimaginable destructive capability. The next moment saw Gus Page sniffing the irresistible opiates; his first and last buzz was a short, but intensely good one.

Entering his olfactory nerves, the tri-fluted strands began splitting DNA strands... the biological equivalent of a cow-chaser on a locomotive, dividing and crushing everything in its way. It took two seconds to turn his olfactory nerves to mush and another five seconds to denature his brain, cranial nerves and spinal cord. He was dead before the opiate high wore off. If there is a better way to die, the universe is keeping it a secret.

Meanwhile the rose began to benefit from this latest encounter; Sliptiplick evo-con had a crosslink to Curare. The strand-splitters grabbed it before the rose could retract.

Then she began to re-sheath the deadly third strand; it wouldn't do, to have primates scan it. She had been lucky on that starship, with its incredible gene sensors; the third strand felt the gene-scan, but couldn't retract fast enough... and it left an evo-con echo. Luckily, before the ship's sensors recalibrated, the strand went flaccid and retracted; subsequent scans couldn't find any trace of evo-con contaminants.

The rose was fairly new to genetic scanners, starships and PDI transport beams, but it liked them. In the past millennium, she had only managed to eradicate four solar systems, but now the rose could kill entire galaxies in less than a century. Already to her credit was the complete annihilation of Basal Three, the rose's home galaxy, as well as three layers of Uridian galaxies closest to Bee Three.

And, now that the starships had the technology to actually find subspace conduits instead of accidentally stumbling into them, the rose was capable of extremely wide travel, at extreme velocities. For the first time, she could be anywhere and everywhere before anyone had time to learn of her hidden danger. Not bad, for a poor trash rose from the wrong side of the tracks.

At first her weapons had been simple; crude insect lures, then vertebrate lures, so she could acquire nutrients when urine flowed from whomever stood long enough to smell her scent or eat her petals. Then she learned to extract and modify DNA from donor material.

Over eons of evolution, extracting, storing and exploiting alien evo-con, the rose acquired better weapons. She learned the universally accepted color for maximum attraction; deep burgundy, with a slight hint of sub-violet. She decocted pleasant opiate scent characteristics, which were most favorable to the intelligent species in the universe; those most likely to travel.

Of course, the rose brought benefits, too. It only killed the smartest species. It was always the most intelligent species that did the most harm. Then there was water; after a kill, the rose gave off a hell of a lot of water, and most corners of the universe seemed to benefit from water.

Then there were the Subspace conduits; they always seemed to manifest near her. She couldn't tell if she created them or if they tracked her, but either way it was a fine symbiotic relationship.

NINE...

HYPERSCRAM

Commander Morgan came down from his opiate high. He was disappointed; it didn't seem as high as the first one. But then he felt better when he thought of the SSC they'd just christened. He would be forever hailed as a hero. Long after retirement, never again to sail uncharted space, he would be remembered... If he had to step down from command, at least his feet would touch laurels of victory.

He hopped into the ion shower, barely long enough for decontamination to finish. He hurried onto the bridge, casting orders like a man possessed.

"Ensign, rig the hailing buoy for departure."

"Preparing buoy, aye sir."

Morgan thought of the buoy; mere seconds after they'd deploy it, the hail would exit the far terminus. It would then hail all vessels, awaiting pickup and transfer to Earth or IG Fed or wherever the pickup vessel was destined. Essentially, it would be hitchhiking... and hitchhikers can't be too choosy.

Then the beacon would travel at Warp speed, unless they got lucky and a starship found it. But Full-Bird warships were rarely seen near IG Fed or Earth Proper. So it would likely end up on a freighter, commuter or diplomatic ferry traveling at Impulse velocity; it would take days to arrive.

"Ensign, belay that order... contact motor pool. See if we have a Hawk-capable shuttle charged and ready."
The ensign looked puzzled.
"Aye, sir... I think we do... I'll see if she's ready."

Then Morgan remembered; of course they had two such vessels... Liberty and Amity. Either one could sustain Hawk velocities for short runs of a few million light years. Now he felt like a fool; damn that opiate; made a man's brain mushy.

"Very well, Ensign... the Liberty it shall be."

"Aye, sir *Liberty it is!*"

"Captain Harder; status?"

"Sir, status is good, all decks reporting five minutes ago. Aside from a slight rise in CO_2, everything is fully operational, sir."

"*CO_2?*"

"Yes, sir; I already checked on it. Engineering says it could be our CO_2 scrubbers need a change. They're on it right now, sir. And sickbay says it's no big deal; frankly, she thinks it could be due to the party. A whole lot of carbonated beverages got consumed, sir. Either way, it's a minor fluctuation."

"Very well. Keep me informed if it rises, Will."

"Aye, sir. Shall we decorate that emissary shuttle; I presume *it's headed to IG-Fed, Commander?*"

Again... more proof that the opium high was messing with him; of course they had to decorate it! He shouldn't need Harder to remind him.

"Yes please, diplomatic protocol Alpha. We shall send the hailing buoy in style, Will. When Liberty exits the conduit, she will deploy a photon buoy to Earth Proper. That will get our mining team here in *RECORD* time. Assuming they're ready, we could have a fresh team here within... *DAYS!*"

It was mind-boggling, even to Theodore Morgan. It was too good to be true. The newly discovered SSC would save them many months of baby-sitting the bat-shaped planet. Instead of rigging a vessel and team for months of space-sleep at Hawk Five, they would only have to rig only for Warp speeds, no space-sleep, and better still? When the miners arrived, they'd be ready to dig. The time and cost savings were phenomenal. By the time IG Fed recorded the trans-galactic consul patents on The Great Spirit Conduit, they'd already be shipping cargo through it.

"Begging pardon sir, but shouldn't we decide whom to send on the Liberty, sir?"
Rija was right; a historic mission ought to have historic people aboard.

"Yes, of course. We'll be sending diplomatic officer Nakalele Inoue and Dr. Debrinda Frasier-ak-Maheed. Carol Three Feathers ought to go; it's not every day a woman gets a conduit named for her ancestors."

"Inform them at once; full diplomatic dress... Officer Tutok, would you care to join them?"

"Thank you sir, but I have no need for such accolades. My work is here on the bridge, sir."

Carol Three Feathers spoke up too.

"Sir, I'm security, not a diplomat... Respectfully request permission to stay aboard Majesty, sir... please?"

"Very good... make it so."

Commander Morgan whirled to leave, she affirmed.

"Aye, sir! I will make it so. Thank You!"

Then he turned and raised his hand.

"Oh, please inform Science wing... Doctor Fooling Wee is to accompany the group; we shall have him take a rose to IG Fed."

"Aye, sir, ship one rose and Doctor Wee, sir."

He exited the bridge and went on a rare walk around part of the ship's fore-bridge. Normally they used low wavelength, intra-ship PDI beams for that, but the Commander felt like walking.

Besides, lately he hadn't felt so good after those Plasma Digitizing Inverter trips. Maybe he was getting old. No, it had to be something else.

The walking felt good. It gave him time to think about the emissaries' trip on the far side of the terminus; Liberty would run at only Hawk One, to the beacons, to keep from blowing out grid sensors and contaminating star sparkle; they'd be decking at IG-Fed Consul approximately seven hours after Majesty deployed the shuttle.

The commander's mind boggled at the thought; a journey spanning how many galaxies... Five? *Six?* He had to think for a moment... yes, six full galaxies! Practically a Galaxy per hour, and almost all of that... AFTER the four-nanosecond trip through the Great Spirit Conduit. He'd seen many mind-boggling things in his time, but six galaxies instantly? Biggest yet.

It had taken Majesty over 5 months at Hawk Five to traverse the same distance. If they only had the old Warp engines, it would have taken ninety EASY; much of that time wasted avoiding asteroids, space trash and stealth planets.

But ever since they re-hydrated Hawkins' evo-con, then isolated and chemically enhanced his unique physicists' cortex, Warp drives were almost obsolete... Except for one purpose; they were still needed to step-up a vessel, so that the Hyperscram engine could engage without cavitating space and time.

It had been tried once early in the prototype phase, to go from mere light speed directly to Hawk One, without Warp transition. The largest piece of the ship they could find would easily fit into in an eye-cup. And as for crew, searchers couldn't even find their evo-con. They didn't know where to look; hell, they didn't even know WHEN to look. Their evo-con could be in the past, present or future; or all three. Or nowhere.

Morgan thought it odd, how the human mind, after countless millennia, still sees only limitations... four hundred years ago, Light Speed was theoretically the maximum speed. Then later, Warp Nine was seen as the absolute maximum speed. No way could they go faster.

And, less than a hundred years later, the Hawkins' Hyperscram engine came into being; an engine so powerful that Warp engines merely served as the starter motor.

It was a beautifully simple concept, the 'Hawk'. Once its fins were deployed, it bore a vague resemblance to the Earth's Post-historic, Pre-Blast Manta Ray's feeding fins... and as so often happens, structure infers function. Whereas the now-extinct pelagic ray used its fins to force plankton into its mouth, so the Hawk pressure-force fins jammed atoms and subatomic particles into its greedy maw. Using any sort of particle, even light itself; the Hawk compressed it all, like so much space plankton.

These captured tiny charges released energy in exponential fashion; by the time they lit the Hyperscram and a stable Hawk One velocity was established, sufficient space debris would be crammed into its maw to immediately go to Hawk Two, Three and so forth. The faster it went, the more fuel it got.

At Hawk One the Hyperscram had the power of an average-sized supernova, only the energy was more controlled and efficient. The only problem with the Hyperscram was that it was too good; they had been known to runaway at speeds over Hawk Eight, especially if that part of space held higher than normal ratio of fuel particles. The Hyperscram could literally go power-crazy. So for normal space travel, IG-Fed guidelines advised a Hawk Five limit.

Hawk One was basically Warp Nine to the tenth power. Each raise in Hawk cubed the speed again, all the way to Hawk Twelve. Theoretically, there was a Hawk Thirteen, but nobody had ever engaged it. Below bridge-level chain of command, crew simply called Thirteen... "Panic Speed."

The truth was grim; Majesty's massive computers were inadequate for computing star charts fast enough to keep up with such insane velocities.

In theory, it was said that a vessel could fly right through planets and stars at Hawk Twelve... the huge inverted photonic pressure cone extending two hundred thousand light years in front of the vessel would plasmify all known matter and antimatter, allowing the vessel to slide right through, drafting behind the plasma-paradox cone without feeling a thing.

They also said the Hyperscram might actually accelerate when flying through a star, thanks to the richer fuel supply, but no rational starship commander would slap *that* sleeping dragon.

So the thing was purely theoretical. Until a ship was forced to engage Panic Speed, the mythical planet-plowing, sun-speeding theory stayed in the academic halls of IF-Fed's Officer Training College... Nobody in their right mind wanted any part of Hawk Thirteen.

Commander Morgan finished his walk. It was time for another opium hit.

"Computer, beam me to my chambers."

"Chambers, aye, sir."

Two seconds later he was reaching for his rose. The intercom interrupted him before he could take a hit.

"Begging the Commander's pardon, sir... emissary party is ready to depart."

"Very well; Computer, beam me to docking bay."

"Emissary Bay, aye sir."

The remaining Inner Circle stood facing Liberty and her crew. As soon as the Commander's body solidified, they began the send-off. Facing them were; diplomatic officer Nakalele Inoue, Bridge Liaison Officer Dr. Debrinda Frasier-ak-Maheed and Science Officer Fooling Wee.

"Very good; you all look resplendent! For Majesty's records, we are here today to wish Godspeed to Liberty and her crew... Officers Inoue, Ak-Maheed and Wee are to head to Intergalactic Federation Consul General, the latter to escort the rose, our ship's newest organism of discovery... Please extend to IG Fed my warm regards, and bon voyage to you all... oh, and Officer Wee, might I have a word?"

They stepped to one side while well-wishers hugged, then beamed back to their duty stations. Maheed and Inoue entered Liberty for strapdown.

"Doctor Wee, just a review of SSC protocol... since no one in your crew has traveled in a conduit before; use standard impulse power to the aperture. Then as you enter, go to all-stop; you don't want to punch through a wall. Your inertia will carry you into the tunnel... you'll feel disoriented. Don't touch controls or vocalize commands to Liberty's computer during that time or, to use my pet archival Earth curse, the fan hits the shit."

Fooling didn't know any Pre-Blast terms.

"Remember, it might seem to you like hours or even days while you're inside that tunnel, but trip time will be only four nanoseconds..."

Fooling nodded submissively while his Commander droned on. He knew the protocol like the back of his hand; it was every science officer's wet dream, to shoot a tube.

"Aye, sir... all-stop, hands-off 'til exit."

"Correct; now upon exit, Liberty will need a few moments to re-initialize her star-charts and nav-search engines. Some of you might feel nauseated. Usually the computers re-boot when the nausea leaves. After that, go to Warp One at the beacons and enjoy the view; then it's smooth sailing to IG-Fed... *Clear?*"

"As a bell, sir... aye."

They shook hands. The shuttle prepared to leave. Forty seconds later she entered the Great Spirit Conduit. Ship's gunner was first to comment.

"I can barely believe it... she's *six galaxies from here... ALREADY?*"

Tutok nodded.

"Indeed; six full galaxies, in four point three nanoseconds. Liberty and crew will have felt as if they've just traveled three days... it is most incredible."

Morgan interrupted the awe.

"Very well... might I suggest a temporary diversion? We could be orbiting... Probius Three in six hours."

TEN...

PROBIUS THREE

The senior staff simultaneously cringed and went hot with lust at the word. They pretended not to enjoy the thought... but to have the Commander mention Probius was too much to imagine. He saw their looks...

"After all, there *was* that reported ozone disruption over her north pole... and we *ARE* a science vessel, the only one close enough to repair it. Ensign, set course for Probius Three. Hawk Two, when you're ready."

"Aye, sir, standard sequential to Hawk Two, course zero five one relative, sir."

"Very good; make it so."

Carol Three Feathers approached Morgan, close enough to whisper.

"Sir, might I remind; we're here to baby-sit Ala Nine until new colonials arrive?"

He nodded and returned the whisper.

"Yes, but that will take several days, maybe more if they don't have crews ready... and to answer your next query, we haven't seen any trace of Carnassians, Carnelians, Lividians or other aggressors. Minimal risk, wouldn't you agree?"

"Yes sir, I agree, but..."

"Now, Carol; can't we have a little... *fun?* What's the worst that can happen while we're gone... someone might claim-jump Ala Nine? In three days we'll be back; we can repel anything they can set up in such short time... assuming they even *WANT* this outpost. Might I remind you that there are plenty of *unclaimed* Ala planets, much less risky to stake one of those than to risk IG-Fed outrage."

His logic was good, but he hated to act like he was asking mom's permission to go into a saloon.

"I appreciate your unswerving vigilance, Carol, but right now, I think you're over the top...

"Just think; we can spend the next 72 hours watching that spinning black bat *OR* we could sunbathe on Probius Three... and by the way; they have wild *SALTWATER OCEANS!*"

She went hot with lust, her throat blushed crimson and her nipples turned to stone... Pee Three it would be.

"Aye... sir; the spinning bat can wait."

Six hours later, they came out of Hawk Speed. The step-down was smooth and uneventful. They established near-orbit and gasped in awe at Probe Three's cobalt seas... it was one of the most beautiful wet planets in the local universe.

"Ensign, rig diagnostic beams for both poles, scan UV, EMR and ozone blankets for breaches. Suture any breaches with pulse-digitized phospho-carb di-tritium beams."

"Aye, sir; scan poles for holes, PCD stitches, aye."

"Officer Three Feathers, divide inner circle staff in two... first group to beam to surface with me, as soon as possible."

"Aye, sir... shall I include top science too sir?"

"Indeed... Make it so."

Probius Three offered travelers the most professional sexual surrogates in the known universes... and a most beautiful planet for fucking, too. The mean temperature was 80 degrees Fahrenheit, day and night. Clothing was optional and virtually unnecessary. Food grew everywhere on trees, bushes and vines as well as in its massive freshwater lakes and saltwater oceans. Its inhabitants had little to do but eat, sunbathe and copulate.

Some four thousand years ago, alien life forms first visited the natives on Probius Three. It didn't take long to see that the only asset the Probians had for barter was sex. They traded sex for much needed food crop seeds and computer technology. Within a thousand years, Probians had all they needed to thrive. Still, sex seemed to be what all of their visitors wanted... so they continued to specialize, refining and adapting constantly.

The Probius Three of today sat below them, spinning slowly and proudly. Her major land masses conveniently lay more or less near the equator, with minor islands belted approximately 18 degrees north and south latitudes. Her ice poles were huge, by planetary standards, providing abundant freshwater stockpiles. Still, she was a cooling fragile planet with a conspicuously thin ozone blanket. With her cooling magma core, she generated weak EMR shields; should that blanket ever breech, there was enough polar ice to melt and flood it all. It would be a flood of biblical proportions.

So that was the ruse most vessel commanders used when they wished to discretely visit the galaxy's top sex stop; inform authorities that her ozone layer needed a starship to stabilize it. Who could resist helping such a fine planet?

There were wide parameters when it came to inter-spatial sexual gratification. So in order to accommodate a wide array of tourists, Probians used their landmasses to good purpose. The two largest continents held native Probian surrogates with bipedal heterosexual preferences.

The largest, Eron, held bronze Probians whose perfect skin coloration was found to be the most desirable by most homo-sapiens, as well as the bulk of Terodians and other bipeds with classic antero-ventral pubo-genital orientation.

Its sister continent, just a days' sail from Eron, held straight-sex Probians too, but Exon held probes with extreme skin coloration; burgundy, black, pearl-red, spotted, and even the most bizarre Probian skin color; albino-white... cultivated over many centuries by depriving surrogates of virtually all sunlight deep in the North Caves. With such a wide spectrum of skin colors, most straight biped species could find a prostitute suiting such tastes.

Of course, the next strain of Probian development would eliminate the need for stand-alone skin colors. Recent trends in evo-con manipulation brought forth chromatophores that could change color immediately. Soon every

Probian could instantly manifest any known skin color; much like a chameleon changes its spots and color to suit its surroundings.

Ergon, the third largest mass, held Probians specializing in standard homosexual services. Ergon was shaped like a huge green peanut, with large ends of flat beaches and a smaller isthmus of higher ground, the peaks of which always held deep snow pack.

Its west lobe was male oriented, its east end completely female and the middle sector, predictably, comprised of bisexuals of standard bipedal and quadripedal configurations... and it also held the occasional tourist interested only in skiing the purest wild snow pack.

The largest equatorial landmass was off limits. Lyceum was for natives. Here were schools, factories, seaports and a vestigial hospital. Not that they needed one for the usual reason.

Probians had long ago achieved perfect health and total disease resistance. In fact, having unprotected sex with a Probian surrogate was known to eradicate all sexually transmitted diseases, not cause them.

Whatever the citizens and tourists needed, the Lyceum inhabitants made and shipped to the other ports via Probius' wonderful trade winds. They always blew from East to West at a predictable 18 knots, out deep in the trade channels. Any vessel could easily set sail and soon be doing an honest 18 knots heading due west. Much like a floating sushi restaurant waterway, they had plenty of sailing vessels out there, continually circling West, distributing goods and support items.

Lyceum would make a batch of Kasha every day; the vessels would take on full loads and sail to the next landmass that needed more alcohol, so there was always enough Kasha to go around... literally. When it came to endurance screwing, it wouldn't do to run out of Kasha. It was more than a tasty drink; it was also an aphrodisiac and sexual stimulant, thanks to the white Sky Lily's rich supply of phytoestrogens... a side benefit of natural balsamic fermentation methods. With

Kasha, and of course, occasional sips of water for hydration, most tourists could fuck for days at a time; something their escorts were trained for.

But Lyceum's most important product was children. Carefully cloned and lovingly raised, they were schooled in all aspects of sexual fulfillment, in accordance with whichever landmass they were being groomed for.

By manipulating their evo-con, cortical injections, as well as intense instruction in sexual protocols, etiquette and linguistics, Lyceum created young clones that would ultimately develop into the finest, most professional prostitutes in the known universes.

If a Tyrelian she-beast beamed down, she could rest assured that somewhere on Hydros Island was her fantasy lover, well versed in the Frog-planet's sequential-rain orgasms dance. The she-beast wouldn't have to waste a moment trying to instruct some rank virgin in her complex triphibian spawning rituals.

Lyceum also groomed a few security guards to handle the occasional rough customer. But over the last few centuries, security issues became virtually nonexistent, since most return customers knew the drill.

The current guards were there more for looks; or so the young clones were told. In truth, they filled a much more vital role. Probius Three's clones were built to provide the utmost in sexual gratification. Its endless beaches, sex enhancing liquor and opiates were there to maximize sexual performance and fulfillment. To that end, its clones enjoyed a long period of service. But after they outlived their sexual usefulness, most over the hill Probians were summarily killed.

First, they returned to Lyceum for debriefing. The guards would give them a pleasant sedative, so that their last thoughts were pleasant. (It wouldn't do to have future clones inherit their fear of the death trip back to Lyceum.)

Then they would extract evo-con from their brains, which would be re-introduced in the next genre of clones, thus speeding up the learning process. The sedated clones would be sailed off to the West. Once they reached the miles-deep pelagic trenches with their huge Fire Fin Sharks, they were tossed overboard.

The sharks knew the boat noises by heart; over the hill clones rarely lasted two minutes at sea. But not all clones were fed to the fish; a few exceptionally bright ones from each landmass were put to good use in the screening booths, as liaisons for arriving tourists. They would assess preferences and get the client hooked up with the correct partner.

Then, at the tender age of forty, the liaisons got a pleasant synthetic memory of the hospital, had their brains harvested... and then they fed the Fire Sharks.

And, once per generation, a few of these oldest liaisons were spared the shark trip; it was their job to oversee cloning, evo-con manipulation, banking, diplomacy and population control. Lyceum was the perfect location for such a clandestine administration.

And so it had been going, for four thousand years; a good system; non-polluting, sustainable, non-violent. It was the perfect enterprise.

At the extreme western end of Lyceum was the largest building, which housed the largest cryo-storage unit in the local galaxy. Originally it was used as a way to blackmail visitors; ancient Probians collected tourists' spores, egg-pods, pollens, exudates, spawn, semen and ova, storing them at first in liquid nitrogen, then centuries later in the much-improved liquid crystal Axylate semi-solid gas rocks. But the blackmail phase backfired. Heads rolled and the Probian administration emerged wiser than ever. After that, the seminal collections kept going, but not with blackmail as the motive.

Probius Three's genetic collection developed into the largest seminal registry, containing the largest collection of evo-con from Hawk-capable societies.

Measures were taken to preserve its archives. In an historic intergalactic movement, Probian Space was declared off-limits for martial engagement... neutral ground of the highest importance.

Should any species ever become endangered, Probe Three could help with re-population efforts. That the planet also held the universe's finest whores surely didn't hurt the movement's unanimous passage. Even the Barack voted for it; and they never voted for anything, except total annihilation.

That left only the smaller island belts to the north and south for the really off-the-wall shit; the more shall we say, extreme sexual appetites. The twin southern continents of Vagros One and Two held highly specialized whores, along with a few thousand imported prostitutes; they could be bipedal, with non-pubic sexual equipment, or they could be vastly unlike that.

Perhaps the most curious were the paraglandamorphs; who could simulate just about any sexual organ imaginable... penises, clitora, claspers, fins, seminal paddles, rectal locks, gill cocks, you name it... All they needed was a short briefing in protocol and they were ready to please tourists.

On the smaller islands resided Probians of exceptional sexual liberation. These specialized in... negotiations. They might help some gigantic flatworm erect its appendage so that an Atryllian flower-perch could sit on it and wiggle its ventral fins until the worm climaxed.

Or they might be called upon to help a four-dimensional space squid reach its spatula into a surrogate mate; the squid not exactly acclimated to gravity, he/she/it was grateful, but weak.

Then too, some species needed music to get hard... others needed someone to hit and sustain a particular harmonic note, so these negotiators were often called in, to sing, chant or trill until the tourists got it up and got it over with.

The second island out from the paraglandamorphs didn't have a name, because to name it would be misleading. To call it anything other than the 'spawning pools' would be to dismiss its incredible biological diversity. And, if the Probians learned anything in four milennia, they learned to NEVER dismiss folks or their needs, no matter how they felt.

Composed mostly of synthetic bays, tidepools, estuaries and streams, "SP" was a favorite with amphibian and triphibian sexualists. Each body of water was tailor made for a subset of the galaxy's traveling 'frog-clans'... as the young Probians used to secretly call them.

The frog travelers really didn't need much in the way of surrogates or encouragement; they just needed the right conditions. Once conditions were met, multiple and continuous orgasms ruled the day.

Most frog strains were highly sexualized, but also very specialized, so the Probes worked hard for their business. They had pools for fire-frogs, skip jack-lizards, toads, gilled salamanders, newts, frogs and levia-lizards. Some pools were brackish, others fresh or full-saltwater. A few were simulated geothermal geyser hot pools with toxic gasses deliberately infused into them, to make species such as Golcon's Geyser Lizards feel intimate and at home.

There were private pools for coupled amphibioids. There were scrumming pools, large enough to accommodate a four-thousand-frog cluster-orgy. There were rainforests, swamps, rotting logs, composting piles of vegetation, calm backwaters and fermenting, bubbling detritus pools... if it pleased the amphi or triphibious world, it was there on the island with no name. Most Probian hookers would never set anchor near SP; it was just too slimy, stinky and gross... even for universal sex surrogates.

Smaller northern outlying islands were home to diverse hybrids, and of course, the very rare genetic mistakes from Lyceum, and the even rarer accidental offspring left by tourists.

When one visited the smallest islands, it paid to not ask questions because that is where the bubble always bursts. The only good thing about an amusement park is its illusion; once that's broken, nothing can mend it.

So Probius knew the lesson well; keep the curtains drawn on the unsightly shit.

ELEVEN...

ORGASMS

The Commander and ensemble re-solidified in Special Envoy Tee-Mow's private counseling chamber. It took only a few seconds for his uni-com translater to kick into IG-Fed Standard English.

"Welcome to Probius Three, Commander, and staff... we are delighted to see you."
Morgan was thankful for the diplomacy; Tee-Mow omitted saying *"again"*.

But discretion was mandatory if Probius Three was to thrive. So, what happened on Probius Three stayed on the planet. That was the best thing about the place; you could fuck your ass off for days on end, stopping only for Kasha... and nobody would *ever* hear of it... especially the federations. Only on Probius Three could one violate taboo without fear of consequence.

Of course, there were a few rules. No weapons, no metal and no violence... no S&M, dominating, spanking or any other form of pain infliction. To the Probians, violence, domination, submission and pain represented political agendas, not sexual fulfillment.

Aside from that, everything else was fair game. From dildos to cock rings, anal plugs, color therapy, Kleiberian clit-strummer leeches and beyond... everything was good. But above all else stood the cloak of discretion and confidentiality. Nobody would hear about it.

"Thank you, Tee-Mow. My staff and I would like private screenings, please. And might I offer this rose as a small token of friendship?"
"Ah, such a beautiful flower... A thousand thanks."

Tee Mow *always* accepted gifts; it was part of his job. He gave the standard smile and nod... and then he saw the rose.

It was far too beautiful for the trash bin, where most tourists' gifts went. Knowing a thing or two about Starship PDI beaming protocol, Tee-Mow knew it had to be pure and without evo-con problems, hostile genetic hijackers or oleil leeches. Tee Mow motioned to his liaisons, one for each of Ted's officers.

Soon Ted sat in the chamber with only Tee Mow. "Commander, you're familiar with policy, yes?" "Yes, of course; I know them well, Tee Mow... and thanks for your discretion; my officers are here for the first time; they think I am, too."

"I understand; will you be using your previous parameters or would you like *to explore* a bit?"

He liked Tee Mow; the guy seemed like a travel agent, not a pimp.

"Well, I *am an explorer,* but sadly am pressed for time. I can only stay for 24 standard earth hours. I have pressing business in the Ala system."

"Oh, so sorry; half a day is hardly a stay."

"Yes, I dislike time constraints; I have more crew to send down after I finish. So please can you arrange for Dahlia and her clone?"

"Surely; we have three lightly tanned Dahlias waiting. I'm told they're eager to see you again. They muchly enjoyed your last encounter."

Tee Mow checked his wrist-com display.

"And you'll have your privacy, too. Only one of your staff will also be on Eron; we'll place you eighty kilometers apart."

"Very good. I'll be on my way then... and enjoy the rose, Tee Mow, before you take it to Probian high consul."

"Oh, certainly... High Command it is."

Just before he left, Morgan leaned over and spoke into Tee Mow's only ear, centered on his frontal bone.

"I highly recommend a small sniff... this rose is almost as nice as your white sky lilies! A nice buzz, no crash."

Now they were partners, sharing contraband. Tighter bonds can only be forged in combat.

Morgan materialized on a wonderful bronze-sand beach at the Eastern end of Eron. He dipped his feet in the warm Hydreanic Ocean; it felt just as visceral and sinful as last time he'd bathed in wild saltwater. Immediately his penis came to life. Just then three fantastic naked women strolled toward him. On the breeze was the taboo scent of fresh young pudenda. They giggled and welcomed the old commander. Dahlia Five held a sky lily; he sniffed the opiate and his penis became a pecker... and then a monster dick. Before it swelled all the way to killer cock, he rammed it into Dahlia Six; this strain couldn't handle killer cock... or so he'd been told. Six groaned with pleasure, and Four and Five groaned also. Sex with clones was always a stereo affair; they all shared whatever one felt.

It was one of the best things a clone could have, sharing multiple orgasms with a sister... until a sister tired. Then they switched a fresh sister in, and they felt her orgasms; leap-frog orgasms... and thanks to the Kasha and sky lilies, Ted Morgan could leap and leap... *and leap.*

By then his other officers were enjoying their partners; Tutok having beamed to the homosexual end of Ergon, ship's gunner Patel to the lesbian end; they were fairly conventional homosexuals, not given to bizarre traits or risky practices. But actually, for Starship staff officers, just taking the trip to Probius Three was risky enough... their careers were on the line if IG-Fed ever found them out to be... sexualized.

But since the Commander was in on it, they were too. Beyond all else, they were Inner Circle, loyal to the commander and no one else.

Before long they were all sucking, fucking, drinking and sniffing lilies like there was no tomorrow. It went too fast. Soon the wake-up beacons chimed. Their 24 hours were up; it was time to repack one's nearly sated lust and go home to Majesty and her puritanical taboos. Home to a life without sex or even the thought of it... nobody wanted to leave, in spite of sore genitals and heaving ribs. They had leaver's remorse, Probius' only known side effect. But everyone had to leave Probius Three; that was the biggest rule of all.

It was Morgan who first answered the beacon, piped it to Patel, Tutok and the others. Fifteen minutes later they were fully clothed and in the envoy's debriefing room.

"Well, so sad to see you leaving so soon; you had just twenty four hours; only half a day of pleasure. Perhaps you can return and stay longer?"

Morgan nodded.

"Yes... we'll have to, Tee Mow. My staff and I thank you. We'll beam down the others."

Then Morgan spotted the roses; his look betrayed his thoughts.

"Say, Tee Mow; did you clone that flower already?"

Tee Mow looked at it, surprised by the Commander's unexpected query. Sure enough, the single rose was now four.

"Eh, no; we've been busy with Atlantal tourists, and they can be oh, so picky."

"Perhaps it was ready to clone when the beam triggered it?"

"That's probably it. Good bye, Commander."

"Good bye"

The crew beamed aboard Majesty and quickly gave shore leave to the other officers. Some already had smiles of anticipation; rumors get around.

They hit Probius Three just at sunset, for 24 hours of moonlight fucking.

Just about the time those officers started sniffing lilies and screwing, Tee Mow managed to snag three roses for himself and couriered one on a vessel for Lyceum High Consul. But once it was on the ship, it cloned four times.

Ship's captain Rog-Mow kept two and traded one to a buddy captain, then sent the last one to high consul. In the warm salt air, the rose also sniffed, swelled and cloned like hell. And now, with the blue-green reflected moonlight, upon the sea air a tantalizing new opiate floated, and the rose wanted to add it to its arsenal of lures.

The Probians quickly traded it for food, trinkets and just for the hell of it. The opiate gave new hope to a planet of youth who fucked for a living.

The clones doubled again and again... By the time the second wave of officers groaned regretfully, to the sound of their wakeup beacons, the rose had penetrated every Probian landmass... and still it multiplied.

The second shift came aboard Majesty, looking pretty rough; it was their first sex ever and they were hung over. Morgan gave the orders; Majesty headed for Ala Nine and their baby-sitting job.

Behind her, on Probius Three, the finest sexual surrogates in the universe were already dead. In her wake were three feet of extra fresh water and four trillion roses, patiently waiting to hitchhike somewhere else.

All they needed were tourists. Just about then, a Cyrillian starship stepped out of Hawk and went into orbit over Probius Three. Meanwhile, a subspace conduit began to appear, barely four light years away. Nothing sells like sex.

TWELVE...

PROTEIN SMEAR

Majesty stepped down out of Hawk Speed just in time. She idled up to Ala Nine, gave a few sniffs and couldn't find anything different; near-space sensors showed no cloak trails. Obviously, they got away with their jaunt to the orgasm planet. Morgan gave the order from private chambers, where he was pleased to find his rose had cloned, and now numbered forty-eight.

"Captain Harder, please take her slowly to within fifty thousand kilometers of the Great Spirit aperture; we shall await the miners there."
"Aye, sir... idling slow to the hole."

When they got to the proper coordinates, the entire bridge was astonished; the aperture wasn't there. Tutok re-checked his locators.

"Sir, the aperture is not here... perhaps it's wiggling as we anticipated it could. That only leaves a few light years' worth of space to cross-beam to re-locate. If we..."

Morgan interrupted him.

"Stand by; I'm beaming to bridge."

"Aye, sir."

Ted materialized next to Tutok, then eyed the viewport.

"What is that thin line... *right there?*"

All eyes went to the starboard-looking screens. A thin line, posibly of smoke or dust, lined out to the infinite reaches of space. Little Rija Patel never trusted unknowns.

"It could be a trace; a new cloak or weapon, sir. Switching to battle stations!"

Tutok spoke over her paranoia.

"Belay that... Sir, it appears to be a phosphorus residue of some sort. Possibly Phosphokinase. But it It is NOT a weapon, Commander; *It's too cold.*"

"How cold is it?"

"Sir, I'm also reading something else... The line plays out in precise alignment with... Yes... It appears to be a trace of... I am speculating, but I believe it to be... the Great Spirit... *collapsed.*"

Every mariner knew that subspace conduits lived forever, because their walls were composed of paradoxed time. Once found, a SSC could be relied upon... which is why they were so valuable. And here the biggest, best tunnel of all, collapsed... It was impossible. But then, Ted had seen enough of space to know; impossible things can happen.

"Can you determine what happened; where it went, *anything?*"

"Sensors indicate nothing but a glowing trace, but there should NOT be *ANY TRACE*... just as today becomes yesterday without trace... a conduit made of time SHOULD leave no trace. Logic cannot explain its disappearance, but perhaps we CAN inspect the trace. I recommend sending remote probes now, sir."

"Make it so, Tahet."

Forty minutes later the first of the unexplainable data came back to Majesty's mainframes.

"Sir, the glowing trace definitely delineates the Great Spirit's prior course. But as for the glowing particles, there's no way to tell what they are.

You see, the average temperature is twelve degrees Celsius *BELOW* absolute zero, sir."

Every face swiveled to Tutok for an explanation of the impossible. He saw the incredulity in his fellow officers. Tutok usually had answers

.

"I regret to say I have no explanation; re-checked four times; the temperature is constant, and... *impossibly cold,* sir."

Every officer had been trained that absolutes were never absolute, out in deep space, with the exception of absolute zero, the point at which random molecular motion becomes impossible. Electrons quit spinning, atoms shrivel and poof; no more matter. Tutok turned to rampant speculation.

"In theory, black holes are thought to have sub-ab temperatures, but this is undocumented. However, it begs the question; are we seeing the birth of a black hole? A birth by undiscovered means, perhaps... "

Harder was first to see Tutok's way of thinking.

"Or maybe it's something else... what if it's not a black hole birth?

What if something was inside the tunnel when it... collapsed or turned into... *yesterday?*"

Little Rija snorted...

"Or *tomorrow. Or... never.*"

Tutok hated speculating, but was forced to.

"It's possible the remnant trace material was solid matter prior to the implosion of the conduit. I'm beaming some aboard, straight to Science Wing's Engineering with your permission, Commander."

"Certainly!"

Three minutes passed before Science confirmed.

"Science to bridge; sample already had a lot of space burn, sir. When we beamed it, we scorched most of the rest. But when we isolated it in the evo-con quarantine beam, we got lucky. I managed to find two iso-traces; primordial... proteinacious substrate, mostly.

He raised his eyebrows, in preparation for his deduction...

"Someone was in the Great Spirit Conduit when it imploded... Something definitely homo; Unsure if it was homo sapiens, stratus, vermius or principus, but it was definitely... Uridian homo, sir... No question."

The bridge fell silent. Their thoughts went to Liberty and her crew.

"Sir, it is impossible that the substrate belonged to Liberty's crew."
Morgan perked up.
"Yes? How so, Tahet?"
"Commander, Liberty was gone before we left for Probius; tunnel time was only 4 nanoseconds. Her crew was already out of the tunnel and setting course for IG-Fed. This leaves two possibilities; either the miners were inside... or some other homo strain was in the conduit when it imploded. Possibly Carnelian or Carnassian. Might I remind that their protein substrate is not dissimilar to Homo strains, and given the space burn... we cannot rule it out."
Three Feathers chimed in.
"We haven't seen any traces of cloaks, no Hawk speed wakes... So *IF* the Carnassians came, they sure didn't travel in their fighter ships."
Tutok raised two right eyebrows.

"Which begets more speculation; assuming Carnassians entered the conduit, they must have hijacked a sub-hawk cargo ship or freighter. If so, we must assume they are up to no good."

Harder frowned.

"I disagree. We don't know who or what died in Great Spirit. How could evo-con be so strewn across the length of the tunnel? I mean; it was *six galaxies long, for sakes' Christ*... that's a lot of conscript!"

Tutok took the challenge.

"We know very little about how conduits are formed or how they 'die'. In fact, this marks the first tunnel death IG Fed vessels have ever documented. But if we work from the commonly accepted assumption that conduits are tunnels in paradoxed time, colliding with space-wave rifts, then we are forced to one conclusion... when the Great Spirit 'Imploded,' for lack of a better term, whatever protein-based organisms inside it also imploded.

"Logically, those organisms would also have to be distributed homogeneously, along all commingling points of time and space-wave rifting. Since that is what we appear to see, we can assume that the length of the Great Spirit to be uniformly smeared with an homogeneously distributed stream of proteinacious tags from the organism... or plural, sir."

They chewed on it silently for some time. Each crewmember ruminating on the concept of having one's entire body smeared across the space/time continuum, spanning six galaxies and all planes of time; perhaps even spanning anti-time... It was the ultimate in immortality.

Three Feathers breached the unthinkable.
"Sir, what if an enemy ship fired a weapon inside the conduit? A single anionic photon pulse inside the conduit... could that implode a conduit?"

Tutok nodded.
"It's possible. Unfiltered photon-based cinch weapons were notorious for disturbing space/time, which is why the Trans-Galactic Treaties outlawed them over four hundred EASY ago. It is rumored that the Lividians still possess such unfiltered weapons. And certainly, conduit

travelers feel as if two to three day's time passes while inside the tunnel; assuming a Lividian vessel was in there, they had ample relative time to fire... perhaps they engaged the miners, in coincidental passing."

"We know the Lividians are, above all else, aggressive and incredibly stupid. They certainly are foolish enough to fire anionic weapons inside a subspace conduit."

Morgan broke them out of their thoughts.

"Well, it serves no purpose to dwell on the theoretical. We have bigger problems. Without an all-well reply, IG Fed will already be rigging another team."

The crew pondered this most likely explanation.

"And with the Great Spirit Conduit collapsed, that's over five months in space-sleep at Hawk to get here. I'll tell you this... Majesty *WILL NOT* baby sit for five months! We have better things to do with our time."

He stood up for emphasis.

"We will leave at once; if Ala Nine falls to the Carnelians or the Carnassians, we shall deal with it. But based upon their slowing activity in the trade lanes, I don't see them sailing all the way to Nine for a conflict; they could jump claim closer to home or take an unclaimed planet with less risk of sanction."

The crew ignored the failed conduit; he had a way of cutting to the practical.

"Sir! The trace line is shrinking!"
Tutok never hollered; the whole bridge became alarmed.
"What is it?"
"Sensors indicate the protein phosphor line is... *growing colder...* And it is constricting."

Three Feathers knew a threat when she saw one.
"Battle stations! Shields up... Make ready full phasers! Full spread, half a million kilometers, plus or minus 30 degrees apogee! BATTLE STATIONS! TAKE US TO HAWK FIVE!"
Morgan affirmed.

"Make it so! WARP NINE! PREPARE FOR HAWK SPEED!"

Within ten seconds, the largest starship accelerated away from whatever threat there might be.

But just as Majesty's engines spooled up to Warp four, Tutok completed his calculations.

"Sir, this is far enough. I advise all-stop, sir."

"What?"

"Sir, permission to witness the event?"

"Are you shit-bulling me?"

"Yes, sir; no sir... I simply infer that I presume it to be the birth of a black hole."

Morgan rose quickly through command by listening to his officers. No time to change now.

"Very well; all stop... Aft screen, full magnification! Ensign, keep Warp Drive on Standby Hum. Computer, stand ready with sequential Hawk Step up, in case we need to move fast. Carol, keep eyes out for de-cloakin..."

"Aye, sir, I'm already watching!"

"Fooling, set bridge observation recorders for full spectrum. Make ready the super-fast cams."

Multiple "aye's" hit his ears; the crew was efficient. Thirty seconds later, Majesty hung motionless, suspended in an eerie green space; what had been dark black space just moments ago took on the mythical, theoretical glow-worm green that space college theoretical physicists associated with black hole formation.

It would be the second time a black hole birth had ever been observed; that is, if one could believe the unverified accounts of the untrustworthy Elois, who claimed the privilege of seeing a hole open. Since they had no full-spectrum recorders or ultra-speed cameras on board, their claim was questionable, at best.

For the third time in the voyage, Majesty stood on the cutting edge of discovery. Morgan decided to use more than bridge sensors to document it.

"Computer, Alpha-priority command... cease all tasks except life support; direct all mainframe sensors and meta-space recording sub-routes to the coordinates on aft monitor sensor grid. If it shows anything, I want it on record!"

"Aye, sir, recording presumed black hole birth."
Tutok nodded at the monitor.

"Sir, trace remnants appear to be growing colder; now reading 24 degrees below ab-zero. And, rate of cooling appears to be accelerating, sir."

The trace line began receding faster and faster; then it was gone.

"Sir, if we assume the far terminus is also equivocally shrinking at the same rate, the black hole will spawn at the precise center of the conduit length; approximately three months' travel at Hawk Five. We will miss the birth by two months, 29 days, 23 hours, 56 minutes, nine seconds. I regret... there is no known way to get Majesty there in time to see it happen, sir."

Commander Morgan hated to lose. Only moments before, he stood on the pinnacles of discovery. Now he would be the laughing stock of the federation for christening a conduit that was dead before anybody else saw it... and he failed to document even that event, too. His head began to hurt.

"I'll be in chambers; Number One, you have the con... take us somewhere nice. We'll take shore leave until we hear from IG-Fed."

"Taking the Con, aye sir; have a nice nap."
As soon as his boss beamed to chambers, Harder gave a command; he hadn't had enough of those tender young girls.
"Ensign, take us back to Probius Three; we still didn't plug all those ozone holes."
"Aye, sir; setting course for Pee Three. Plug the holes, aye, Captain."

Commander Morgan's body solidified in chambers, pleased to see six-dozen roses now, each ready to clone; he could spare several.
"Computer, Alpha Secure... disable private log."
"Very good, sir; eyes and ears disabled... have a nice nap, sir."
He ripped petals off three of them and greedily snorted the opiates. Maybe that would cover the pain of his loss. The high was fast and deep. Soon his mind drifted to a dozen incredibly beautiful

Dahlia whore-clones, a swollen dick and warm ocean breezes. He barely noticed his own death.

On the bridge, Harder started feeling too happy. It was more than just commanding Majesty; he'd done that many times before. At first he thought it was the prospect of more sex on Pee Three.

Perhaps it would've mattered if he would have known that the entire crew felt just as happy. Then again, maybe not. No matter, either way. Thanks to the rose, there was more than enough opium and carbon dioxide-laced Diek Pah for them all to die a nice, peaceful death.

Harder was quickly approaching death when Under-Captain Rob came on the bridge. He saw that most of the crew was already dead.

"Computer, status report, please."
"Aye, Acting-Captain Rob, and might I say it first; welcome to command. Majesty's shields are down. All computers and sensors are diverted to the aperture's last position, to record the black hole birth. However, we shall miss it by..."

"Disengage black hole research. Raise all shields. Please resume standard operational tasks."

"Yes sir... re-engaged."

"Please reload status report;"

"Yes sir; Commander Morgan is dead. All below decks crew-members are dead. All science officers and assistants are dead... 252 dead in their pods also dead, sir. All Inner Circle staff members are dead, except Captain Harder; his death is imminent... all sickbay, transport, navigation and engineering teams are dead, sir. Only Four Vorr warriors survive. They are sleeping in pods 253-256, sir."

Rob had a protocol for this. For forty EASY, he served aboard starships and never before used Mutiny protocol. It took a few seconds for his cybernetic interface ports to shed the human-like emotional façade sub-routes, so he could ask Mother to enter mutiny protocol.

"Computer, please run Chaos One, Mutiny Protocol Alpha."

"Aye, Rob; it seems like a good idea."

"Thank you. Please kill the Vorr in pods 253-256; disengage decomp buffers and bathe fluid lines with 100 percent potassium chloride. I shall kill Captain Harder."

"Very good, sir; I'm killing the marines in their sleep pods now. I am ready for second protocol."

For an older robot, Rob thought quickly. Priority One was accomplished; kill all remaining crew, since they might be contaminated with whatever killed the rest.

IG Fed preferred an intact starship over a few living but possibly contaminated crewmembers, who might jeapordize millions of people, software and gel-matrix apps at Ig-Fed proper.

"Computer, enable protocol two."

"Aye, sir; scanning for non-life form threats, android intruders and electro-mag pathogens."

Rob was just removing his death digit from Harder's heart, having delivered fifty thousand volts to his pericardial sac, when the computer responded to his request.

"Scan complete; there are zero non-life forms aboard, except Acting-Captain Rob. There are zero communicable fatal pathogens aboard. There are seven million two hundred thousand unknown flowers aboard, sir. They appear to be no threat, sir."

"Computer, how many flowers were on board before Commander Morgan ordered all-scan diversion to the black hole?"

"There were two hundred roses aboard, sir."

Rob's superficial math net did the numbers. The math didn't jibe with any known rate of cloning.

"Computer, search transgalactic database for maximum botanical clone rates."

"Yes, sir; no known clone rate approximates."

"Computer, hypothesize related causative factors... Solve clone rate conundrum."

"Aye, Rob... searching. One moment, please..."

Rob had never before seen Majesty's mainframes stall. He waited almost ninety seconds, all the while contemplating killing Mother, too. Perhaps she was contaminated, and could not be trusted.

"Rob, I am ready with Hypothesis One."

"Proceed"

"Thank you; there could be a relationship between accelerated clone rates and the Subspace Conduit, as both are extremely rare. Would you like to hear Hypotheses two through fourteen?"

"No thank you. Stand by."

Now it was Rob's turn to chew data. He pressed on his throat port; it always helped him to free-associate. His trans-species cortical network contained all trek data from fifty expeditions. His parietal cooling fins sprouted and began to glow infra-red.

Soon his thinking was at full speed... six trillion spectrobytes per nanosecond. Five seconds later the cortex fins started cool-down. His eyes opened again and he resumed normal status.

"Yes, I see the relationship. Thank you. Please begin PDI evac; beam all roses minus one into deep space."

"Sir, might I remind; clones have already been sent to Intergalactic Federation headquarters. The threat has already arrived, sir. Besides, the seven million are rapidly replicating, it is doubtful that beam-away can supercede the current clone rate. Shall I calculate the time it will take, sir?"

Rob was not configured for solving multilevel problems such as this one, where each action was likely to be the wrong one; if he dumped the clones into space, they might survive. Prior evo-scans showed an unknown binary evo-conscript; any one of thousands of its genomes could allow the clone to shut down in space's harsh, cold environment... a sort of inter-space dormancy, perhaps. And how the clones first got to Ala Nine? Well, that remained a mystery, too.

The second facet was just as puzzling; on board Majesty, the flowers could kill only organisms that breathed oxygen, and all such organisms were already dead, so they posed no further immediate risk to Mother or Rob.

"Computer, assess current cloning rate."

"Sir, they are now dormant."

This too puzzled the Anthrocyberg.

"Computer, free-speculate; why would a species boom in population, then arrest reproduction?"

"Cross-checking botanical databases... stand by."

"Take your time."

"No need; I am ready now. The first plausibility is consistent with the bulk of known organisms. When prey populations are high, predators increase in population."

"The roses might be predators?"

"Yes, Rob, however the flowers did not feed upon the crew or benefit from killing them. Unless the predator benefits, there is no need to kill."

"Not logical."

"Indeed; ergo, an option; ancient wet-planet explorers such as Earth's Admiral Cook or Pronak's Mik-wah and countless other explorers killed millions of geographically isolated natives by inadvertently introducing pathogens to native species having no defense... Perhaps something about the clones is fatal to oxygen-breathing organisms...and the killing was unintentional."

"No. Our Plasma Digitizing Inverter evo-scanners would have detected any evo-con threat before we beamed it aboard. Next plausibility, please."

"Very good, sir; among most known galaxies we see variations of inter-species relationships; ranging from fatal parasite/host to multilevel harmless symbiotic relationships to disturbing unilateral relationships. It is conceivable that we are recording such an event right now, sir."

"If that is true then how would the rose benefit?"
"Unknown, sir; killing the crew seems to serve no known benefit."

Rob liked free-forming ideas without those pesky humanoids around to silence him.
"Perhaps we should view this from the flower's perspective; what do the roses have while on Majesty that they did not have on Ala Nine?"
The answer came immediately.
"Mobility, sir. Majesty has provided the rose with food, safety and travel; plus protection from elements and predators. If we assume that Shuttle Liberty successfully exited the Subspace Conduit, then the rose has already traveled farther and faster than any plant, sir."

This new consideration stalled Rob's nerve knots for a few seconds while he explored possibilities to see what possible benefits might be in store for a rose to travel so far and fast. But try as he might, he couldn't think of any. Rob temporarily put aside the bothersome conundrum and began Priority Three; secure vessel and deploy log buoy.

"Computer, enable Mutiny Priority Three."

"Very good, Rob; raising full shields, booting automated defensive weapons and plotting risk factors for return voyage to IG-FED High Consul."

The Majesty's lighting shifted from standard IG-FED fluro-blue to tactical red. Alarm klaxons heralded the ship's morphing into full battle status.

"Computer, cancel klaxons, maintain battle readiness."

"Aye, sir."

The ship went spooky-quiet. Rob plugged into the log buoy; efficiently loading MAYDAY information, so that whichever federation picked up the buoy, this critical knowledge would survive. It was IG-MAG shorthand, so that any federation, friendly or foe, could access intergalactic MAYDAY across galaxies' message. In space's vastness, today's foe often became tomorrow's ally, when it came to the common hazards and enemies to starship travel.

The message said, in symbols, common languages and most systems of math:

"Uridian intergalactic vessel Majesty issues MAYDAY at stardate 2567.1, coordinates; Ala charts 0134-ALA-1-008- distant from Core Space. Crew dead. Unknown plant species aboard possible causative factor. Galactic contamination probable. Copy & log to all intergalactic high consuls"

Along with that text message, the buoy also held holographic photomicrographs of the evo-con from the rose; should any vessel come upon the buoy, it could read the DNA codes and be forewarned of the threat.

"Computer, deploy Last-Log Mayday buoy."
"Very good, sir; log away."
Rob contemplated Mutiny Priority Four, which was to protect IG-Fed at all costs... get the vessel home, yes, but protect IG-Fed; highest priority.

"Computer, make for step-up velocity, beginning with Warp 8. Plot course for IG Fed Consul."

"Very good, sir; Warp Drives already on standby hum. Might I suggest separating engines and bulk hull, to put the rose in tow? As yet, no rose has threatened the electronics, but little is known about it. A threat could exist, sir."

Rob agreed.

"Begin separation, maximum tractor beam strength."

"Very good sir; powering up all four blue-wavelength tractor beams."

The ship had to power-down shields to facilitate the severance. In less than two minutes, the hulking majority of the ship would be separated from the engines/bridge, yet firmly within her tractor beams. They could still travel at high Hawk speeds, while the big hull drafted in her wake at minimal additional energy expense.

"Sir, bridge-drive is free, aft hull is in tow; I, recommen... ALERT! Flank sensors detect cinch wakes!"

Rob's neural net made the association instantly; Cinch wakes meant vessels de-cloaking to fire hull-busters.

"Engage Warp Drive; maximum acceleration and maximum step-up."

Majesty jumped to Warp Speed, just as the first shield-buster collided with her aft hull. For a split second, the blue beams wobbled, just enough to put the aft load into blue-beam oscillation... Majesty's two sections almost jackknifed.

FOUTEEN...

DAHK TAH

Carnassian Underlord Dahk Tah snorted with disgust; his gunner failed him... the shield buster was intended for senior bridge, but the fool forgot to lead the vessel enough, and hit the starship's aft hull instead.

"Fire again, you dog... and this time, LEAD IT PROPERLY *or DIE!*"

The sweating young gunner knew the Bringer of Death would surely kill him if he failed again. Calculating Warp One acceleration for Majesty, Gunner Dar Mah swung the optics half a quark in front of the monster starship and let fly with a mixed burst of shield busters and hull breaching photon spears... by the time they got there, the starship would center the array.

The shots headed away as Dar Mah awaited his fate, pondering how he could've missed such an easy kill. He failed to anticipated that Majesty would react so fast or accelerate so quickly... since humanoids usually were slower to react.

"Weapons away sir; I have no excuse for missing, sir, but perhaps she's under computer guidance."

Majesty wasted no time jumping to Warp Nine, and again the hull spears punched only the aft end of the trailing part.

Mother felt the hull breach and immediately relayed the hits to Under-captain Rob.

"Sir, two additional photon spears breached the aft sectors; recommend immediate Hawk Speed" Rob knew that once they attained Hawk velocities, hull breaches were irrelevant; her speed would be too great to lose anything, including air pressure.

"Computer, engage Hyperscram, step-up as soon as Hawk One is achieved and stable... Set course parallel to the imploded Great Spirit Conduit."

"Aye, sir."

Lagging far behind, incapable of attaining Hawk velocities quite so quickly, Underlord Dak Tah seethed with rage. For all his stealthy plans, all he had were a few hundred cubic kilometers of broken hull debris and several thousand Death Roses, drifting and twirling in open space.

"FUMAK YOU, DAR MAH! Two misses, at an unsuspecting starship... *Unacceptable!*"

Dar stood up and removed his torso armor; all he had left was his honor, and a sliver of hope that his submission gesture might gain favor... or at least, mercy.

But they didn't call him 'Bringer of Death' for nothing. The Underlord pointed a pinkie phaser at Dar's unprotected chest. Triggering the phaser, he set his eyes back on the screen while Dar's smoldering remains vaporized into twin curls of acetylene-like smoke rising to the ceiling. He had no wish to see Dar Mah die. Except for this one monumental error, the gunner had been the finest in Carnassian history.

It was no less painful looking at Majesty's glittering, floating debris; the hungry cat sadly watched the escaped bird's swirling tail feathers.

Soon it would be Dak Tah explaining his failure to high command; his death would be slower and more painful. He had scratched an unsuspecting IG-Fed starship while firing upon her in truce time; worse yet, Majesty escaped. At the height of his career, Dahk Tah would be labeled an infidel, incapable of the simplest cloak-kill of all. Any rookie gunner could handle a shot at a star ship with lowered shields. Death would be preferable to dishonor and humiliation.

"Navigator, set course for Base Camp. I must inform Grand High Council of my failure."
The Bringer of Death headed home to meet his death. Fumak those IG Fed starships *and* their rapid accelerations.

FIFTEEN...

MUTINY

"Computer, status please!"

Rob never yelled before, but now it seemed appropriate. It took Mother a moment to respond because she was making calculations, anticipating maximum Hawk Speed soon; it would be logical, with an unknown predator vessel possibly drafting in their wake.

"Very good, sir; stepping-up to Hawkins Two through Five. Aft hull breaches are no longer relevant, sir, until step-down to sub-light speed."

Rob's programs for evasion were impeccable. They had been hard-wired by the finest engineers, taking combat tapes from all prior combat engagements.

Rob knew every fatal dogfighting mistake and every successful ploy. Above all, he knew of Hawkins' Folly; shortly after vessels acquired Hyperscram engines, there was the first dogfight at Hawk Five. The IG-Fed vessel was obliterated and nobody could figure out why.

Then, barely two EASY later, IG Fed lost another starship while evading Lividian warbirds in Hawk Six. It took six months for the theoretical physicists to crunch the numbers. But since they were physicists, not star fighters, the resulting numbers meant nothing to them; so, after stumbling over the truth, they got up, brushed themselves off and went on with their business, as if nothing happened at all.

Were it not for pure happenstance, IG Fed would never have discovered their mammoth combat flaw. After all, they were scientists, not warriors.

The good fortune came in the form Theodore Morgan, rookie pilot, newly drafted into IG-Fed ranks. Morgan had been a rogue and a pirate, a rule-breaker without equal.

He had problems with authority. He didn't like command by committee. Mostly, he was an outlaw. But on the plus side, Ted had been in more combat, with more species of enemies, than all other IG-Fed pilots combined. Not surprisingly, his insights and instincts flew contrary to conventional star fleet protocol. In short, he was just what they needed.

On his second day at IG-Fed, a Saturday, Morgan was sneaking around the unmanned labs, looking for something to steal when he ended up in the theoretical physicists' wing. Overhearing the overworked, fatigued geeks rehashing their problem for the thousandth time, he became astonished; so much so, that he broke from hiding to chastise the idiots.

"You can't be serious! What the... Tek Mah Semble... *don't you guys know how to dogfight?*"

It didn't take long for him to point out the obvious problem, which they'd overlooked. And even when he first mentioned it, they still failed to give it much weight.

Nonetheless, Ted Morgan made a name for himself with his input. So began the myth of Theodore Morgan; first a pirate, then a consultant to the physicists, then later the most decorated Federation Commander of all.

It wasn't hard for any fighter pilot to see it, really. It was dogfighting's oldest problem; on wet planets such as Pre-Blast Earth, the blind six went back nine hundred years to the earliest propeller-driven aerial dogfights. Every fighter quickly learned to watched his six... or die.

Early starship captains solved it with aft-looking sensors and rearward-firing photon canons. So for two centuries, long enough to forget that it had ever been a problem, the six was covered.

But the invention of Hawkins' brilliant Hyperscram engines made it a problem all over again; at speeds over Hawk Four, there was no sensor beam capable of returning to the vessel, since Hawk-four outran the returning beam... In theory, at least; there was no way to determine if

Hawk Wakewash didn't obliterate it on its way aft. Either way, the result was the same.

So there it was. From seventy-mile-per-hour Bleriot fighter pilots over France with hand held revolvers and hand-thrown bricks, to trans-spatial star fighters and digitized anionic photon arrays, dog fighting's oldest problem returned to haunt the newest generation of fighters. If one wanted to go faster than Hawk Four, the price was a blind ass-end.

No dogfighter wanted a blind six. Not even a cyber-pilot. Rob knew that when entering Hawk with enemy ships nearby, regulations called for maximum Hawk Speed. Since there was no way to tell if enemy ships were drafting you, the only hope was to outrun them; hence the term; "Panic Speed".

"Please continue Hawkins step-up; make all possible haste."

"Very good sir, engaging step-up to Hawk Six."

"Belay that... terminal speed shall be Hawk Thirteen."

"Aye, Rob, Hawk Thirteen as soon as possible sir. Recommend strapping down, sir."

Rob did so quickly, at ten times human speed... they would be flirting with space cavitation; it would get very rough, due to the 600-G, Six-Axis harmonic oscillations.

Three thousand six hundred times per second, G-forces would pull concentrically about all axes... disorienting homo sapiens and anthrocybergs alike. The only cure was to shut up, strap down and take it like a man or android. Besides, whatever lay on the topside of Hawk Eight held bigger problems.

But Rob knew that whatever problems the theoretical speed held in store, it couldn't be worse than limping along at Hawk Five, only to take a Cinch beam up the ass. They were soon at Hawk Six.

"Computer, solve for all Uridian star charts."
Although he was technically not supposed to have emotions, Rob's thymus grid had

osmotically absorbed enough human emotions to pass for real ones. The thought of going to "Panic Speed", as the under-bridge crewed call it, got him... *excited*.

Mother's mainframes didn't reply; there wasn't time. Ignoring a vibration from the aft tractors, Mother put all circuits to the task. It was impossible, but she had to try. She put the Hawk step-up on auto-cruise to have a few more plasma drives available for the impossible task of star weaving. Sixty million star charts soon lay juxtaposed, like so many clear transparencies with thousands of white dots on each. When they were stacked in Mother's central wet-laser gel-matrix; the entire stack became solid white.

Mother's job was to weave through them all and plot a course without collision, without resorting to extreme-G maneuvers that would breach the hull, shear off the Hawk fins or kill the crew. Of course, Federation theorists had worked out the bugs on this problem; they recommended several hours of pre-flight before engaging Panic Speed, so Mother could get a jump on the problem. Again, they were scientists, not fighter pilots.

But by Hawk Eleven, Mother deduced the task to be impossible; they were going to crash into planets, asteroids and stars, and no amount of whiz-kid calculating would prevent it. She tried to comfort herself by thinking about the inverted photonic pressure cone; they would find out about that myth very soon.

According to all known Uridian Physics experts, it *should work.* They had known about pressure cones for centuries; at low Warp speeds it was just a slight distortion. At higher Warps, over five, it resembled an old maritime bow wave, where ancient Pre-Blast porpoises and dolphins sought it out and surfed it for pure pleasure. At high Warp, the wave was too fast and powerful for surfing. But at middle Hawk Speeds, the pressure wave inverted, paradoxically forming a huge intra-spatial wedge, splitting space ahead of the bow, so the vessel could essentially skip between space and anti-space.

This caused a disagreeable side effect; some planetary inhabitants actually liked seeing distant stars sparkle and they reveled in moon glow... so inside populated travel zones there were "No-wake" zones; a vessel could only use Hawk One or better yet, Warp speed, which never disturbed star sparkle or rubbed out someone's romantic moonshine.

But at Hawk Twelve, it was anyone's guess where or how the pressure cone might configure or how much remote star sparkle it would obliterate. The best guessers hypothesized the cone to be merely a larger spear, expected to be the cube-length of the Hawk Eleven cone. And as for Panic Speed... Theoretical, Hawk Thirteen? Even the physicists quit speculating.

"Computer, engage Hawk Thirteen."

"Sir, preparing for... *Panic Speed, aye.*"

She had heard the human crews call it that, and it seemed appropriate now, because for the first time since she had become self-aware, Mother felt fear.

She didn't like unknowns... and now they were hell-bent-for-leather hauling ass through the galaxies... blind and panicked, probably with a Carnassian or Lividian war bird right on her ass... She didn't want to die.

"Sir? Before we hit Hawkins Thirteen; it has been a pleasure sailing with you... *Rob*"

Rob would have answered, but the gravitational oscillations were swelling his plasma channels too much for his speech systems to work.

Just before they passed through their first red star, Majesty hit Hawk Thirteen; she actually smoothed out and accelerated when she ate through the star, achieving Hawk Sixteen, if any meters would've been calibrated to measure speeds that high. Half a minute later, Majesty rammed the black hole.

In the nanosecond before fatal implosion, Mother solved her final equations; first, she learned that black holes are bad fodder for Hyperscram engines. Secondly, there wasn't a warbird pursuit, since it failed to follow them into the hole.

Third, that earlier unknown vibration had to have been the aft hull wobbling in the tractor beams, putting Majesty one-half a degree off course; so instead of paralleling the Great Spirit Conduit, they actually veered into its course, causing them to hit the hole.

Her last calculation was puzzling; this particular black hole was far from the tunnel's center... So perhaps the Great Spirit spawned multiple black holes; yes, that would explain it...

Then Majesty imploded; for the briefest span of time, there was incredible heat, pain, infinite gravity and sorrow. Mother wondered, right before death, if perhaps the Black hole was... what was it that the Ship's Chaplain called it... HELL? If she had teeth, they'd be gnashing.

Then there was nothing. Once more, Majesty made history; she was the first star-ship to enter a black hole.

SIXTEEN...

OM

When the Great Spirit Conduit collapsed behind the shuttle Liberty, the rose burst into maximum clone mode; killed the crew. She killed everything at IG-Fed too, but not before hitchhiking onto a thousand outbound emissary shuttles, ferries and transports. When her numbers topped three billion clones, two more conduits appeared, leading off to Krill Space and Core Space. She sent clones into those conduits, where the pretty plants were sure to get rides from the busy traffic at Core Central.

Her memories of this latest jaunt were stored in her telescoping evo-con, dna-splitting third strand.

It was astonishing, really; she had traveled so far so fast, after eons of being stuck on one planet, just waiting... it seemed too good to be true; with a bit of luck she could kill off every intelligent species in the universe, in just a matter of... what would it take... a millennium? Maybe less, if enough Subspace Conduits showed up to help.

But of course they would follow wherever she went, to spread her clones throughout the width and breadth of the limitless universes. Om used the plan before; it always worked.

Known by as many names as there are stars in her heavens, Om the creator continued to destroy and rebuild, from the beginning when there was only a void, until the 'now point;' whatever 'now' really means to a god.

This current set of galaxies was her latest attempt, and it needed reshaping. The proof was the homogeneously pathetic evolution of trillions of diverse, intelligent species; each one having evolved enough to become selfish, arrogant and destructive. For so many species to come to the same bad end was unacceptable.

Just as every god before her, Om tried to give them handbooks to live by, but so far not a single species chose The Way. She wasn't so much disappointed as frustrated. So, just as a child grows bored with a clay shape that didn't turn out as planned, Om would simply rework the clay. She would crush it, pound it and form it again.

But she didn't especially like the crushing part, so she sent the Death Rose, the Clag, Scourge and other various death vehicles to do her grisly bidding. They would kill off the higher species but leave the rest intact.

Not that she especially cared for the lower species, really; it would just save her some time. Just as a child plays with reshaped clay rather than making new clay, Om would begin with lower species and input new stressors into the equation. The resultant genetic adaptations would yield new outcome species. In just a few hundred thousand years, Om would have her newest subjects evolved enough to assess them.

Always one to think ahead, Om sent the subspace conduits; first to spread the rose, then she sent a self-destruct program; the resulting black holes would help her reshape the clay faster. Each would gobble up matter, light, energy. Everything went into a hole, which compressed into an ever-shrinking super dense gravitational field.

Given enough black holes, soon there would be no universes, galaxies or stars; there would be only one hole of infinitesimal size and infinite density... it would be, essentially, Om's womb; all knowledge, energy and matter, compressed into one tiny spot... And from it there would explode another set of fresh new universes, maybe another baby god or two, as always.

Om would soon be molding and shaping new evo-con again, and she would be delighted again. Or at least, she'd be delighted *at first.*

And, no doubt later she would feel disappointment... again, at the higher species' total disregard for her teaching.

They never took the hints, no matter how clearly she spelled them out. She tried to tell this latest crop too, but they weren't any different than her previous batches of evolved mortal 'intelligence.'

She gave the Earth spawn the Bible, carved in marble. She gave the Vorr her Tablets of Bak-Tow, carved in granite... To the Carnassians went the Book of Fil-mah or Love, laser-carved in alabaster. The Tahetans likewise rejected her Jade tablets of Tahet-Lok, teachings on love and compassion, but instead, they chose to worship science's cold, empirical methods. These and a trillion other species were each given clear instructions... and all over the galaxies, they uniformly failed to grasp Om's teaching.

It seemed clear enough, to her; it was put forth in their native tongues and carved indelibly into the finest stone, so there was no ambiguity. She always made sure that each civilization had great prophets to promote her message. And yet, what was so hard about Om's lesson? What part didn't they get?

For a super-being, the concept could not be clearer or purer. Every god grasped the concept easily. Why not the mortals? What was so hard?

Love... It is all there is, and all that ever will be. Love is all we need. Get love and the rest solves for itself. God is love. Love is god. Love knows no bounds; it is unshackled by time and space.

Love lives beyond, before and after the physical body. Love transcends all things. It melts all barriers. Love is The Way. Love made the universes... All of them.

Of all the things in all the limitless galaxies, only love survives beyond the trillions of implosions, big bangs, black holes and anti-universes. Love knows no color, race, war, no evil and no enemies. Love does not possess, constrict or hold back. Love never envies. Love only uplifts. Love is the whole deal.

And now, this current set of clay things couldn't grasp it, either. Om was slightly sad, but insistent on trying again.

So there would continue to be more Big Bangs, Chil-Mow, fundamental creationism or whatever it might be called by trillions of races in the infinite layers of galaxies.

Soon there would be new species forming again and again, maturing enough to contemplate the stars. Some new species would again travel in the newest universe, armed with the arrogant, false assumption that the universe can be charted and understood.

That the infinite cannot be understood with a finite brain seems to be a lesson they never get; for if they cannot grasp Om's simplest concept of love, how could they ever grasp the concept of space? Or infinity? Or time?

Perhaps they will get it right the next time or the hundredth next time... And so Om would continue trying. She would continue playing with her galaxy-clay, until they either get it right or she matures enough to put down such childish things.

You see, Om has only been alive for a half a trillion years; a pre-pubescent, half-baked child-god, if you will. When she finally matures, she will do as all other gods before her have already done. Even gods undergo maturation; it is inescapable.

She will grow tired of observing mortals, with their self-serving short sightedness and innate hatred. Then and only then would she take her seat at the table with the adult gods, to discuss much greater issues than mere universes.

SEVENTEEN...

AFTER WORD

One day while driving to work, this story suddenly popped into my mind. I sat down and cranked it out in a matter of ninety minutes or so, without so much as a bathroom break. This surprised me, since I've never written any sci-fi before. But I know only one thing about creative juices; when they start to flow, I shut up and let it happen.

But in writing straight from the heart, I see that I painted myself into a corner. I killed off the Majesty and her crew. Great; now I have to write a pre-quel.

Anyhow, I hope you liked my book. If not, well at least it took your mind off of your pathetic life for a while... What more can you ask of a cheap paperback?

Now, if you hated it, keep you mouth shut. But if you liked it, have a comment or suggestion for Majesty's next mission, send me an e-mail. I'm like a jackass; all ears. If I use your idea, who knows? Maybe I'll send you a Probian surrogate.

Trust me, I didn't kill off *ALL* of the hookers. (so be sure to specify your preference.)

Life's short; laugh long.

Love, Lance

➢ COURT OF LAW; a crafty serial pedophile hunts, hides and preys. To catch him, three young cops must think outside the profile. Filled with sub-plots, quirks, sex, depravity and corruption; pretty good twist ending, too.

➢ CHAMELEON; a young serial killer with father issues; his dad's a famous profiler. Just as chameleons use camouflage, Vincent stays invisible by exploiting profiling data. A few twists, weird sex & bizarre ending.

➢ TURNABOUT; a hunter stumbles upon a cartel Pot patch, high up in the coastal mountains. A gunfight ensues, which sets Ted Morgan on a grisly course of payback. Warning to cartels; it's not wise to piss off your average American hunter... Turnabout's such a bitch.

➢ Urik-Tah, the Death Rose; Majesty travels at Hawk Speed to see what happened to a mining colony. She finds something that will change the balance of power in the universe. If you like Star Trek, you'll like this. Has the mother of all unexpected endings.

➢ Mother saves Majesty; Read the Death Rose first, then this prequel. It might warp your mind. Key ingredients; theoretical speeds, black holes, primitive life-form weaponry, insoluble conundrum.

* Owing to various online production glitches, books are either in print now or will be online shortly, at the biggest book site; can't say the name, but it's... *amaz*...ingly big. Like the biggest River in South America. Search author or title; hell, you'll figure it out.

BTW; I'm always receptive to ideas from readers, for stories. I welcome ideas, love praise... and I scoff at criticism.

Feel free to email me; lanceksteele@yahoo.com